I0791868

KISSES AND WISHES

WILLOW WINTERS

WALL STREET JOURNAL & USA TODAY BESTSELLING AUTHOR

From USA Today bestselling author, Willow Winters, comes an exclusive collection of novellas!

Romantic. Addictive.
Second chance wishes and first time kisses. Everything you need for a cozy read.
You'll devour each of these winter reads down to the last page.

The previously released stories available in this collection are:

One Holiday Wish

Collared for Christmas

Stolen Mistletoe Kisses

One Holiday Wish

CHAPTER 1

CARLA

The light dusting of snow steals my attention as it blows in the bright lights of my headlights and across the sidewalk. It's dark already, even though it's only six, but I'm wide awake with the nervous butterflies in the pit of my stomach.

The sound of the keys jingling is all I'm left with as I turn off my car and sit in the driver seat. Rustling in my bag, I find the stick of sheer berry lip gloss. It matches my nails that I just had done yesterday too. I spent way too long thinking about what I was going to wear. It's just a holiday party, and hosted by my best friend, Lauren. So it shouldn't matter.

Every other Saturday I park my car right where it is now, and head straight into her house without an ounce of makeup on and only in my PJs. I have no shame when it comes to girl's nights. And a holiday party of just close friends normally means making sure I'm wearing real clothes, complete with a bra – even though I hate bras. Not the designer skinny jeans and flowy white silk blouse I picked out just for this night.

My phone pings with a text from Lauren just as I'm smacking my lips together: *You here yet?*

Just pulled up.

My phone buzzes again with: *Shit, I have no red wine!*

My lips quirk up into a grin as I snap a picture of the two bottles in my passenger seat and send them to her with the line: *Got you covered.*

You are the fucking best. My smile widens but with her next message, it falls.

Now get your ass in here!

Deep breaths. Dropping my phone into my bag, I open my car door and grab a bottle of wine in each hand which means I have to bump my car door shut with my ass.

It thuds as it closes and so do my heels in the bit of snow.

My coat's not shut tight enough with the loose tie, but even with the chill, I'm burning up with nerves.

He's going to be there. I swallow down my anxiousness as my heels crunch down the snow and I get closer to the front door. I can hear the laughter, the chatter, the faint sounds of Christmas music.

I should be excited, - *merry*, so to speak – but I can't shake the apprehension, knowing Michael Davis, my high school boyfriend, my college on-again-off-again-can't-keep-my-hands-off-of-him-when-we-run-into-each-other-occasional-fling is going to be there.

All of these nerves because of one very important detail.

He's coming back home; he's moving in down the street from me, back into his old house. It was one thing when I could travel a thousand miles and put distance between us after we had a rendezvous. It's completely different when he's a block away and we'll run into each other constantly.

I don't know how I'm going to keep my hands to myself. I don't know if I want to try to pretend like I don't still want him.

Ringing the doorbell, I tell myself the scary truth that has me shaking in my cherry red heels, I don't know if he wants me at all now that he's back. That's the part that makes the butterflies in my stomach beat their wings a little too hard.

CHAPTER 2

CARLA

"It's irrationally hot in here," I tell the back of Lauren's head as I plop both bottles down on her kitchen table, knocking the bowl of Tostitos ever so slightly.

"Wine! My hero," Lauren drags the "o" way too long as she gives me a hug without wrapping her arms around me because she's got a Solo cup in each of her hands.

"You started without me," I jokingly scold her and slip off my jacket as someone comes into the kitchen from behind me.

"Pre-gaming was like hours ago girl. You and that bakery," she's back to filling the cups as soon as I let her go.

"I'll be in that bakery every day until I die," I respond

and my words are full of pride. It's my family's bakery and I'm the one who inherited it from my grandmother. My mother's a nurse and my father married into the family with a career in law. So the bakery – and all the memories that come with it – are all mine. "I wouldn't have it any other way."

Lauren rolls her eyes at me but then winks and gives me a nudge to look behind.

Shit. I almost say the word out loud; I wasn't ready for this. I should be or maybe I should know I never would be. But dammit, I thought I'd at least have one minute... to down whatever is in that Solo cup in Lauren's left hand.

Michael is standing right there behind me, telling something to James that makes him laugh as the two of them open the caps of their beer and toss them in the trash can next to the counter. As Michael lifts his beer to take a swig, his eyes catch mine.

My heart pounds in my chest.

The second he lowers his beer; he smiles at me. Charming, sweet but he fails to hear whatever James said. My floosy of a heart picks up her pace.

"Are you listening?" James questions Michael, clinking the bottom of his beer against Michael's.

"What?" Michael's attention is stolen by James and it's only then that I let my own smile show. Even though

I know the blush will stay right where it is and I won't be able to hide that.

"Dude," James shakes his head in disapproval until Michael nods slightly my way. I see him do it and stupidly, I stay put, a hand on each bottle of wine as if they'll save me from this awkward moment.

The movement doesn't go unnoticed and Michael lets out a soft chuckle before pulling his bottom lip into his mouth and biting down on it slightly, shaking his head at me.

Instantly, those butterflies move lower, so does every bit of heat in me. It's his broad shoulders, I think, that does it. Lauren and I narrowed it down based on my celebrity crushes. The way he hovers over me, dominating my space and closing me in. I am a helpless victim to it.

And that lip that's trapped in between his teeth right now, I'd like to bite it too. In fact, I have. On multiple occasions.

"Carla!" James is the first to speak. He and Michael roomed together at college. He knows every sordid detail of what Michael and I have done, and unbeknownst to Michael, he also kept me up to date when I wasn't there, filling me in on any and every detail of any girl Michael could have gone after. He never did date anyone else though, even when I broke it off, admitting that the distance was too much. He had school. I had the bakery. It wasn't going to work.

But James and his wealth of information are the reason I always fell into Michael's bed whenever Lauren went to see James, her brother, and she needed a travel companion, or whenever Michael came back here, to this small town. James is the one who told me I was all Michael ever talked about and said he didn't want anyone else.

I didn't want anyone else either. But when we hooked up that first time after the break up, I didn't want to put a name on what we were. So it was on-gain, off-again, whenever we were around each other, or miles away. Just hooking up, but I didn't want to hook up with anyone else.

"Hey, I heard you were coming back," I say off handily, peeking up at Lauren to save me, but she's busy gathering a bag of chips from the cabinet.

"So that's how you're going to play it?" Michael's question catches me off guard.

"What do you mean," I play innocent and peek at James just as Lauren bails on me, practically running out of the kitchen with a twinkle of mischief in her eyes and the widest smile I've ever seen. Michael asks James to leave us for a minute and before I can even turn around, we're alone.

"So you don't want them to know?" Michael asks and I stumble on my answer.

"Know what?" Adrenaline races through me. We've never talked about what we do and I sure as hell don't spread the gospels about how I still spread my legs for Michael.

It only takes three foreboding steps from Michael. One. Two. Three. Until he's standing over me, invading my space and making me crane my neck to look up at him. I can smell him, feel the heat radiating from him. I could taste him and that lip of his if I wanted to right now.

"That I fucked you last week on my sofa... and then my desk. And that you already know I'm coming home because I mentioned it before you left."

"They don't know." I answer him with a shake of my head. Michael's facial expression gives no hint of what he thinks about the fact that I kept it a secret. Whether he likes that I've kept it a secret or otherwise. His statement is simply matter of fact ... and dripping in sex appeal. Until he clarifies with another question.

"So you haven't told anyone?" His eyes flash with something. It's gone as quickly as it came, and too soon for me to place it. Maybe guilt? I feel it too. Everyone in here knows what we used to be and I don't want them coming between what we have now simply because I'm happy with the way it's been. Even if we don't have a title.

Or I was... until he decided to come home. Still, we don't need the opinions of the peanut gallery.

If my nerves would calm the hell down, if I could breathe whenever Michael gets close to me, I'd be a better fighter in this battle of flirtation. But as it is, Michael dominates every piece of me the second I smell his woodsy scent, or see that dark stubble that lines his sharp jaw all the way down his neck.

"You're staring at my lips, Carla," Michael's voice is deep and husky, and the way he speaks sends a heat straight to my core. "You want something?"

I only nod, and let my fingers reach up to the last button on his long sleeved Henley. The deep groan that slips from him is accompanied by a roar of laughter from just on the other side of the wall in the living room. Lauren's house is small, it's all her own, but this is a tight space to hide something like what I want to do with him.

"You want to go upstairs?" Michael asks me, glancing behind him and I follow his gaze. No one's there but the shadows of people are coming.

The second I nod, his hand is on mine and I creep up the stairs of Lauren's two-bedroom townhouse as quietly as I can. "We won't have long," I whisper and wish I'd had at least one glass of wine so I can blame this on that, but the way Michael looks when he pulls me in closer to him at the top of the stairs has me drunk on lust already.

"We can be quick here," he leans down to nip my bottom lip before adding, "And then we have all night."

CHAPTER 3

MICHAEL

I missed the slower pace of this town and how everyone knows everyone.

I missed being able to walk everywhere and know that every single building has a story to tell.

I missed all of this when I left for college.

But most of all, I missed her. My Carla.

Pushing my hip against her belly, I back her up until her back hits the wall. Grabbing her wrists in my hand, I pin them above her head. No one can see us here, but if anyone came up the stairs, they'd have a view of everything.

Carla moans into my mouth and my cock is instantly

hard. I rock it against her, making sure she can feel what she does to me.

She breaks the kiss before I'm ready, leaving my heart racing. As I trail my finger down her arm, still keeping her wrists pinned, I watch the goosebumps spread across her body and her nipples pebble through that thin bra and loose blouse she's wearing.

"Did you wear that for me?" I ask her and my voice comes out huskier than I meant. I have no control when it comes to Carla.

She nods and pushes herself against my leg, grinding into me. "All for you," she nearly whimpers as her back bows and she rocks herself harder against me.

Releasing her wrists, I cup her pussy through her jeans and my other hand goes to her hip. My lips trail down her neck until I can nip the lobe of her ear and whisper, "I need to be inside you in the next two minutes or I'm going to lose my shit."

Carla's eyes widen, as if registering what we're doing for the first time. Her lips purse as she glances behind us, to Lauren's bedroom. "We can't. Not in Lauren's room and the other is where her sister is staying."

I back up slightly, wishing a third room would appear when I see the wide hall closet. So wide it's two-doored. Not hesitating, I swing the closest door open and pull a string to turn on the old light. There are only a handful of coats on left side and plenty of room on the right to take care of Carla and the hard on that never goes down when she's near.

"I need you to be quiet," I warn her and open the door wider. it's not until she takes one last peek down the stairs before she grins at me. A mischievous and sexy grin that has my cock aching to be inside of her.

"I can be quiet," she whispers and lets out a giddy feminine laugh as I come in behind her. "Liar," I tease her and close the door behind me.

Before her back even hits the wall, her lips are on mine, sucking and nibbling. I don't waste any time either, pushing my hand up her blouse and rolling her hardened nipple between my forefinger and thumb.

She moans, loud, breaking our kiss and I pull back on her nipple in punishment since I know that mix of pain and pleasure is delivered straight to her core.

"I bet you're wet for me," I taunt her in a low breath.

"There's only one way to find out," she teases me back and as my hands find the button of her blue jeans, she does the same to mine.

The button, the zipper, the jeans in a mess around our ankles.

I groan in the crook of her neck as I tear off the thin lace that separates her hot cunt from my fingers and learn that I guessed right. "You're so fucking ready." I leave an open-mouthed kiss on her throat and then on the back of her neck as she turns around for me, slowly and with intent. It's more difficult with the jeans still around her ankles, but she does it well like the little minx she is.

"We've got to be quick," she whispers as I wrap my hand around my cock and stroke it.

"I should have stopped by the bakery before coming here." I'm only joking, but the serious side of Carla comes out when she answers me, "Not going to happen in the bakery."

The smirk on my face is uncontrollable. "That's what cars are for, baby." I playfully answer and smack her ass before telling her, "stay quiet," and shove my cock inside of her in one swift stroke.

Fuck, my eyes nearly roll back into my head. Not just because she feels like heaven, but because of the look on her face right now. Eyes closed and her mouth open with a silent scream of ecstasy.

With every buck of my hips, I brace her against me so her body doesn't hit the wall.

I could give two shits if they know we're fucking up here, but I know Carla doesn't want anyone to know.

I'm sure they're thinking we're doing something else right now. That I couldn't wait to ask her. And that's fine by me if that's what they think. They should know better at this point.

"The two of us can't be in the same room together without getting inside each other's pants," I whispers to Carla and as she smiles, I slam inside of her. Again and again.

She's trying to grab on to anything at all, but there's nothing but bare wall in front of her.

It's hard to control myself as I slam inside of her, still bracing her against the wall. Feeling her cum around me, the heat, her arousal, the way her cunt grabs my cock. Fuck. I'm going to cum and I'm not ready. I want to fuck her how she likes, rough and hard. For hours.

"Tell me I can have you again tonight," I barely groan the words out at the shell of her ears and she shivers, shivers from her shoulders and down, all the way down, in a way that leads straight to my cock.

"You can have me," she gives me just what I need and lets her head fall back against my chest. Her cheeks are full of color, her lips still parted and her eyes half lidded.

"One more," I whisper against her heated skin and reach down to rub the rough pad of my thumb against her clit.

Her hands come up to her mouth; she bites on her thumb to keep from screaming as I fuck her recklessly, harder, faster, waiting to feel her cum one more time.

The second she does, all the tension in her body

leaves her and I feel my own release with her. Gripping onto her with a bruising force, I let go of everything and cum with her, feeling my balls draw up and the tingling in my spine. My toes curl as the pleasure rocks through me in waves.

I can barely breathe I cum so hard.

I pull out of her, wishing we had more time and use her underwear to clean her up and then shove them quickly in my pocket. She's still panting against the wall and I have to help her pull her jeans up. I have every curve of hers memorized. The way she leans her head against the wall is exactly how she does it on my pillow. And her fingers come up to rest in the little space below her collar bone, that little divot she loves for me to kiss. She does that every time too.

Time ticks too fast. I want to stay in this moment forever. But that's a holiday wish that won't be gifted.

"Is this going to be something we do one last time? I don't know that I can handle..." Carla asks me quietly, one hand on the doorknob and the other on my hip. Her eyes reach mine, and I hate that she has any insecurity. It's always been her. I knew if I didn't push, I'd hold on to her until I could come back and be here for her how she wanted all these years.

"Carla, I have one question to ask first."

My heart hammers in my chest. It's now or never. As

my bottom lip drops to ask her the one question I need answered, the door to the coat closet flies open, bringing with it the bright light of the hall way and a not-so-shocked Lauren who somehow manages to bother grin and scream out, "I knew it!" at the same time.

Fuck.

CHAPTER 4

CARLA

"Everyone!" Lauren's screaming through her house with a shit-eating grin that won't budge. The thud, thud, thud of her pattering down the steps as quickly as she can is far faster than mine because of these heels.

"Lauren!" I scream her name and add, "Don't you dare!" as I bend down on the third step to grab my heels so I can catch her barefoot before she can go shouting to everyone what she just saw. I have half a mind to throw them at her as she lands on the bottom step.

"Guys!" Lauren squeals as she rounds the corner, leaving me in a view of only her hand. My chest is heaving in air by the time I catch up to her in the small living room crowded with James and four more friends for years and years. Friends who have been my family and know every detail of my life. Including the bits about Michael. The very large bits that have made up most of my life since the tenth grade.

All of their eyes are on me, I can feel them burning into me as I hold up a heel at Lauren, ready to tell her to shut it just as she announces, "He totally gave it to her already!"

Gave it to her. My mouth drops just like the shoe in my hand. How could she? Betrayal rips through me like I've never experienced in my life and instantly tears prick my eyes. Were they betting on how long it would take before I fell back into bed with him? Fuck. That hurts more than anything ever has. Embarrassment doesn't even register. It just hurts.

"Lauren, I didn't ask yet!" Michael's voice booms down the stair case. I barely notice the thumps pounding down the steps and coming up behind me.

"Fuck," Lauren covers her mouth before closing the distance between us and grabbing my shoulders. "That sounded so wrong. I thought you two were up there because he asked you. I'm so sorry. Don't take those words like the way they sounded.

"You really put your foot in your mouth," James laughs at Lauren, no sense at all

"I thought he asked her!" Lauren raises her voice and directs her guilt on James who shakes his head comically. "You're a mess," he jokes and my friends in the room chuckle. Everyone still jovial as if nothing's wrong in the least.

"Ask me what?" I breathe the words and turn around to face Michael, his soft blue eyes piercing me like they always do.

"Oh my God he's going to do it now," I hear Lauren's words rush out of her mouth as she steps away, giving us room and letting everyone else see the two of us.

My heart beats fast, my body heats and my lungs stay perfectly still, refusing to let me breathe as Michael takes my hand with one of his, running the rough pad of his thumb over my wrist and reaches into his pocket to pull out a small black velvet box.

Oh, my fucking God.

My bottom lip wobbles slightly as my eyes glance at the box, then back to his eyes.

Michael lets out an uneasy breath, "I wanted to ask you in private." He clears the nervousness from her voice with a small cough before continuing. "I wasn't sure what you'd say, but I guess in front of all of our friends is a perfectly fine way to do it."

"You remember how you asked me what my holiday wish was?" he asks me but my mind still isn't functioning quite right and I can only stare back at him, feeling so much excitement, nervousness, so much hope that this means he wants the same as me. Michael glances at everyone behind me before leaning forward and reminding me, "Last week when I saw you, do you remember when I asked you and then you asked me back?"

Blinking away the buzz of this frenzy I nod vigorously and Michael smiles at me, it's a lop sided grin that makes him that much more charming. "You've got to help me here," he whispers just for me, "I'm nervous."

Rocking onto my tip toes I steal a quick kiss from him, feeling the blush rise into my cheeks, "Sorry, I swear I'm paying attention." He laughs as I rock back down onto my heels and look up at him with a warmth flooding every bit of me.

"You're my holiday wish." He stares into my eyes. "I just want you and this can be whatever you want it to be, if you want me too." His words come out faster as he goes on until he takes a moment to breathe, opening up the small velvet box for me to see. "A promise ring or more, I'm not sure," he lets out a long breath as I peek at the sparkling ring.

Tears cloud my vision of the rose gold diamond ring with floral details surrounding it. *Or more?* I never expected this.

"I'm not sure what you want, proposal or a promise, or to get married tonight. I just want you and this is for you."

"Tonight!" the word shrieks with glee from behind me and I look over my shoulder to see Lauren barely being held back by James. She covers her mouth with both hands and I have to laugh at her antics. She's always said we were meant to be together, that even a thousand miles wouldn't keep us apart.

"Not tonight," I say mostly to get that thought out of Lauren's head before looking back at Michael. "Not tonight," I repeat and hold his hand tighter. "And if it means I get another, this is just a promise ring," I bite down on my lower lip to keep my grin at bay, but it doesn't work.

Michael's shoulders shake as the tension around us eases and our friends laugh from my answer.

"Told you!" this time it's James who pipes up.

"I'll get you another then." Michael's voice is soothing, and the look in his eyes is everything right now. Devotion, love, the way he looked at me when we shared our first kiss, our first time, all of our firsts. And the way he looked at me when I left him, thinking I couldn't be the only one who felt this between us, but too scared to ask. "When you're ready."

"Let's just be us, for now."

"That's all I want."   He lowers his nose to mine, and gives me another kiss as the chatter and cheers pick up behind us. It turns to white noise when he whispers though, "I love you Carla. I always have and I always will."

My lips press against his for a short kiss and then I whisper in the warm air between us, "I love you too."

Collared For Christmas

CHAPTER 1

JOSHUA

I sigh heavily at my desk knowing I shouldn't be doing this. But I fucking want to. I lean back in the leather chair, staring across the room with the tips of my fingers tapping on the Mahogany desk.

It's been years since I've seen her and now that I've had a glimpse of my sweet cherry, I can't get her out of my head.

What's worse is she didn't even see me. Or maybe it's better that way. I'm not sure.

It was her voice that made me turn. The soft cadence that spilled from those beautiful lips. Had I never heard her, I wouldn't have seen her. It's incredible how sometimes fate gives you just enough of a glimpse to change everything.

I close my eyes remembering the sweet sound of her voice. She ordered a salted caramel coffee and a blueberry muffin to go. I huff a small laugh at the memory. She always had a sweet tooth. Her pale pink, A-line dress flowed below her hips as she moved across the glass display case, smiling sweetly as the young man handed her the muffin.

She nibbled on the muffin as she waited for her coffee. Those plump lips parting ever so slightly as she pushed a stray crumb into her mouth and sucked gently on her finger. She'll never know just how tempting and sexy she is without even trying. The sight made my dick twitch. I remember how she wrapped those lips around my cock and owned me as she sucked me off. I groan in my chair trying to push the past out of my mind.

I was stuck there, in my seat at the far corner of the coffee shop, frozen in time, watching her as though I weren't really there. The paper in my lap and an espresso on the small, white table in front of me, I stared at her with desire.

I couldn't believe she was there right in front of me. As if the time hadn't passed and we hadn't parted all those years ago. I sat there in awe until she accepted her coffee with a smile, taking a sip as she strode to the front, shifting the purse on her shoulder as she pushed the door open and left, blending into the hustle and bustle of the city.

I smile at the memory, back when we were together, she never drank coffee. It doesn't surprise me that she ordered it flavored and added so much damn sugar to it.

I had no idea she'd moved to the city. I had no clue she was anywhere near me. *My Cherry.*

I'm ashamed to remember how I followed her to her office building. The winter air blowing in my face and the Christmas carolers already out in the morning on the corners of the busy streets. I walked into the sleek skyrise with shiny steel and tall glass windows. I've driven past this building a thousand times. I remember thinking there's no way she's been this close to me all this time.

I walked in behind her and watched as she walked through the marble floored lobby of Parker-Moore and confidently strode towards the elevator. I walked to the fountain in the center of the lobby and watched as she took small bites of what was left of the muffin, waiting for the elevator to ding and take her away from me.

I look back to the screen on my computer. All of her information is there. Alena Morgan. She's a chief advisor for a prominent sales company now. After years of schooling and a prestigious internship. Now she's back. Back in my life with her dreams accomplished.

And according to her background check, her name is the only one on the lease.

Which means she's single. As far as I can tell she is.

I fucking hope she is. I want her now even more than I wanted her then. I knew I'd hold her back, I knew she needed more from life than what I had to offer back then. Fuck, we were only just experiencing life and I wanted to keep her all to myself. I felt selfish and like an asshole for making her feel like she needed to run. And when she walked away, I let her go without fighting.

The day she left me tore a hole in my heart, filled only by my work. I worked in private security with a good friend of mine, Isaac. Every fucking day, I was working. Trying to ignore the fact that I'd let her slip away.

She was mine. Had I told her no, she wasn't leaving, I think she would have rebelled, but I could have disciplined her and she would have fucking loved it. She would have seen how good it felt. How much she wanted it as much as I did. We could have made it work. But back then, I wasn't the man I am now and I sure as fuck wasn't the Dom I am now.

She wouldn't have understood her feelings and I would have failed at explaining them to her. She was degrading what we had by thinking her submission made her weak. It doesn't make her any less of an equal to submit. If anything she has the upper hand. I'm the one who needs to know the limits, her limits. The limits that *she* sets.

But she didn't accept that. She wouldn't. She left me and I let her go, burying myself in work as a punishment more than anything else.

Until I met Lynn and created this place. *Club X.*

A smile curls my lips up.

I never dreamed it would grow to be something so ... powerful. This lifestyle has always been a passion of mine. The darkness may have been hidden and subdued, but it's always been there. I didn't know how lucrative my expertise would turn out to be.

This rebuilt mansion is an escape to debauchery and sin for the rich and powerful. Our security and use of non disclosure agreements as well as the clientele make Club X unique and desirable. We're exclusive and that makes the members even more eager to join. Most only know of Club X through word of mouth. We don't have a website and we aren't interested in advertising. With a ten thousand per month membership fee, we don't need more business.

This club may be my profession, but it's so much more than that.

It's something I want to show my cherry. I know she'd love it. She's the most submissive woman I've ever met. She's confident and professional, but she craves an escape from responsibility. She loves handing over power to those she can trust. She may not be aware of it, but it's liberating for her.

I need that exchange of power. I need her back in my life.

I haven't had a steady relationship for years. I haven't even had a submissive or played downstairs for months. I haven't *wanted* like this in so damn long.

Not since she left me.

I click to my email and hover the mouse over send. But I can't do it. I can't let her know that I'm here just yet. I'm afraid she'll run.

I stare at the screen, feeling pissed off to even be in this predicament. I know one thing for sure, as soon as I get her in here, I'm not letting her go.

At that thought, an idea strikes me.

"Lynn?" I call out of my office and my business partner, the face of the business really, peers into my doorway.

We met years ago and hit it off right away as friends, good friends too. We aren't anything more than that, and we both like it that way. In this line of business, that makes what we do much easier.

"What can I do for you Joshua?" she asks, walking in but only taking a few steps into my office.

I don't want my sweet Alena, my Cherry, knowing I want her here. I want her to come here on her own.

I tell her, "I need you to send an email for me."

She tilts her head with her forehead pinched, "am I your secretary now?" There's a touch of humor, but also slight disbelief.

"It's an invitation and it can't come from me." I tap my knuckles on the desk, debating on whether or not I should tell her.

Judging by the smile on her face, she doesn't need to know more. Lynn is an expert at judging facial expressions and apparently I've given more than enough away.

"I'm happy to help," she says with a twinkle of mischief in her eyes.

CHAPTER 2

ALENA

I swallow thickly looking up at the large wooden doors. This is for me. A Christmas present of sorts for myself. I'm finally going to go through with it. My heartbeat races and my palms are sweaty. I've never done anything like this. I haven't even been with a man in years.

As pathetic as that sounds, work has taken priority. I'm more than ready for this.

I had a boyfriend, Joshua, years ago, who made me want this. He was my first in every way. He teased me with the idea of being a submissive. Really, I teased myself. He wanted me to kneel, to crawl to him, to obey his commands and let him tie me up. I'm wet just thinking about him and his dirty words.

I was convinced that lowering yourself to be submissive was wrong and dirty. That it was degrading.

But I'm obsessed.

Even more, I'm turned on by the idea.

"Come here Cherry, be a good girl for me," his seductive words echo in my memory and I have to close my eyes and sink my teeth into my bottom lip. My heart clenches at the memory, so does my pussy. Joshua was good to me.

But he didn't last. Your firsts never do. We each wanted different things and moved on, going our separate ways. It was hard at first, even if it was my decision.

After all, I was falling for him, I was weak when I was with him. I craved to submit to him and I know how badly he wanted it. But I wasn't ready back then. I didn't know that I ever would be. Almost ten years later, ten years wiser and more established, now I know what I want.

And now I'm standing out in front of Club X. It's not well known. It's full of powerful men and rumored to be the hottest BDSM club there is. But it's secretive for a reason. From outside it almost looks like a mansion. It's large and intimidating, but aged with beauty. There are details in every aspect of the architecture and landscaping.

It's a gorgeous building, but I have no idea what it looks like inside. Pictures are forbidden. The only ones I've seen are from the emailed invitation I was sent.

And I certainly didn't focus on the architecture in those pictures.

I almost didn't open the email. I had no idea who Madam Lynn was and it's only out of curiosity that I clicked. It was a personal invitation. Somehow she knew what my dark desires were.

My blood heats at the memory. It's been two weeks since I got the email. Two weeks of warring with myself. But I'm a grown woman. I'm successful and I have everything I've wanted out of my professional life. But my love life is non existent and I don't even know how I'd find a boyfriend.

Nor if I'm interested in one. But I can't deny my curiosity.

It's only two on Tuesday, so I'm sure it won't be packed. I'm surprised they're even open.

I wanted to see what it was like on my own. I just want a small peek to see if I'm really tempted. I want to know if I can actually do this. The thought of being a submissive is intoxicating; it's a fantasy. I don't know if I can go through with it. But I have to try in order to find out.

I ball my hand into a fist and knock against the door. The cold air makes my knuckles hurt at the hard contact. It's only when I'm pulling my hand away that I see the black cast iron knocker.

I roll my eyes at my stupidity. But before I can dwell on it, the doors open and I sucked in a breath.

A large man, opens the door. I have to crane my neck to look him in the eyes. I am a step lower than him, but still, his broad shoulders and towering height are intimidating. He's handsome enough, but not really my type. He looks down at me and cocks a brow, "Are you a member?" he asks. "I don't recognize you," his eyes travel down my body, "and I'm sure I would had I seen you before."

"I-" I almost stutter from the nerves, my cheeks heating with a violent blush, but I clear my throat and grab a hold of myself. I shake my head, "not yet." I'm proud of how firm my voice is, but my heart is trying to climb up my throat and my body is humming with anxiety.

This is my choice. I can always leave if it's not what I expect.

"Welcome," he says with a smirk on his face, opening the door wider and allowing a warmth to flow through the door, urging me to enter.

Seductive music lures me inside. I give him a small smile and blush again when I catch him blatantly staring at my ass. My heels click on the stone floored foyer. The ceiling is domed and there's a large desk to my right, a coat check on my left. Beyond the foyer, the deep red carpet mutes the sound of my heels as I step forward, drawing me to the large open ballroom beyond the lobby. Or is it a dining room? There are tables and what looks like a stage behind a thick velvet curtain. I unconsciously step forward drawn in by the elegance and mystery and, to be frank, disbelief.

It literally takes my breath away.

"Miss?" A woman calls out after me. Her voice breaks me out of my reverie and I turn to face whoever's calling me.

A gorgeous woman walks towards me with a confidence I can only wish I possess in the boardroom. Her blonde hair is pulled back into a bun and her makeup is flawless and natural with the exception of a slight cat eye and thick long lashes that must be fake. There's no way those are real.

Although she's not young, she has a better figure that most and she strides towards me in her Louboutin heels as though she's owning a runway, the scarlet colored dress clinging to her curves the entire way.

Madam Lynn. She must be the Madam of the club.

I take a step forward and hold my hand out, moving my coat to the crook of my arm. "Madam Lynn?" I say, although it's a question.

The woman pauses, accepting my hand and smiling with a twinkle in her pale blue eyes.

"You've finally come." She says accepting my hand shake and taking me in. "Alena, correct?"

I nod my head and return her smile although my heart's still pounding in my chest. "Yes, I'm here."

"I'm glad you've accepted the invitation." She looks at my coat and then back to my eyes. "May I?" She asks while reaching out for it.

"Oh sure, of course." I hand her the coat and she immediately takes my hand and leads me back out into the lobby.

"I know you're going to want to look around and," she looks over her shoulder at me with a mischievous grin, "have some fun." She stops at the desk and waves over a young woman in a silk black jumpsuit, "but let's get you checked in first." My cheeks color with slight embarrassment.

"Yes, Madam Lynn," I say just beneath my breath.

She looks back at me with slight surprise and tilts her head. "Oh he was right about you."

I take in her words, letting them resonate in me slowly, as she walks behind the desk with the other woman tapping on keys at a computer.

Who is 'he' and what the fuck was he right about?

CHAPTER 3

JOSHUA

I watch on the screen in the security room as Dominic let's Alena in from the cold and takes a deliberate look at her ass. It would piss me off if I wasn't feeling so fucking confident.

She's here because she wants this. She wouldn't have come otherwise. She had one day off this week and she chose to use it to come here.

I should be ashamed that I hacked into her emails, but I'm not. It's something that's almost natural at this point. With every application we do a background check. And that includes some digging that's on the other side of the law. But we have to be careful.

And with Alena, I had to make sure she was single and that she was still the same woman I once loved. The thought strikes me like a hit to the chest. *Love*. It's been a long time since I've said that word. With no family and no relationship, I haven't had a reason to. I huff a small laugh as I realize the last woman I ever told those three little words just walked into my club.

I remember her whispering it with such sincerity after I took her for the first time. It was slow and sweet and I hadn't revealed how much more I needed from her. I was desperate to have her and I wish I'd told her sooner. Regret starts to creep up on me, but I shake it off.

She's here now and that's what matters.

I watch the screens in the control room as she walks into the dining hall. She's beautiful in her cream chiffon pleated dress. She looks innocent and naive wearing that in here. If it were any other time, she'd be struck with surprise at how out of place she is. We usually don't let anyone into the building this early. Some Doms have keys to the private rooms that work from the entrances outside, but not in here.

When she emailed back asking to come, I allowed it. I'm already breaking rules for her. I'll break them all to get her to submit to me.

Madam Lynn is getting her set up. Watching the two of them interact makes me uneasy. Lynn knows how much this means to me. I turn on the volume for the mics and listen in as they walk through the hall and into the play rooms. There are several on the first floor, and even more in the dungeon.

Alena never struck me as a woman who'd care for the dungeon. She doesn't want pain. She just wants to give up control. Even if she doesn't realize it.

My thumb rests on my bottom lip as I watch the screen.

They're quiet as they walk into the first play room and she eyes the Andrew's cross in the back of the room.

There are two crosses as well as some other furniture meant for BDSM interaction.

I can see her tied to one. Bound and helpless. Her eyes widen slightly and I can see her breath hitch as she realizes that's what it's for. She pauses mid step and looks at the dark raw wood beams as though they may bite her.

I lean forward watching her every move and willing her to explore.

I don't want her to be scared off just yet. She would enjoy it.

As if hearing my thoughts, she takes a few steps forward and gently touches the wood. Running her fingers down the side of it and eyeing the leather cuffs attached to it.

I can see the wheels turning in her head and finally, those plump lips part with lust clouding her eyes. *Yes!*

She turns abruptly and clears her throat.

"How are the…" she looks away and then back at Madam Lynn. "How do the Dom's choose their subs?" she asks. My skin prickles with excitement.

"Well," Lynn takes a seat on the dark brown leather chaise and crosses her legs as she leans against the back of it. "Submissives and dominants are free to roam so long as they're wearing the bracelets that signify their interests.

"So as long as I have no collar and wear this," she raises her arm, showing off the three layered bracelet, silver, black, silver, bands. "Then the dominants will know?"

Black for carte blanche. A smile slips into place. I have so much to explore with her. So much to teach her.

Lynn nods her head. "That's correct." She gestures to the cross. "If you'd like to go up there, you can simply kneel by it and wait for a partner.

Alena's head whips to the side. "Just wait?" she asks with a higher pitched voice. Her face is etched with insecurity. "What if no one wants to."

Lynn laughs at the absurdity. It pisses me off that she thinks no one would want to accept the offer. She'd have men lining up for her.

My hands ball into fists. That's not going to happen though. I'll kick all those fuckers out before I allow that.

She's mine.

My anger dissipates entirely as Alena asks, her voice laced with fear, "what happens if they just leave me there or-"

Lynn's quick to cut that off, and I'm relieved she's there to put cherry at ease. This was good. I was right to handle it this way. Lynn isn't intimidating in the least. This is the perfect introduction for Alena.

"We have security in each of the rooms at all times. All you'd have to do is safe word. If you're gagged, then you can use a hand signal."

I can see Alena taking in the information and letting it calm her down. She nods slightly and looks at the other trinkets and toys around the room. Most items are in packages because of the nature of their use. Vibrators, plugs, nipple clamps. Some paddles and whips aren't packaged. They can be wiped down and sterilized.

"You can always go up for auction," Lynn offers out of nowhere. Every hair on my body stands upright, the breath stolen from my lungs. Once a month we hold an auction. It's a one month long contract. Lynn's eyes meet the camera in the room and I know that comment was meant for me.

I grunt and sit back in my seat. Fuck that, cherry's not going up for auction .. although. If I bought her she couldn't say no. I'd have her to myself for an entire month.

She'd have to sign the paperwork afterwards though. And the next auction isn't for two weeks. I'm not waiting that long or risking her running when she finds out that I'm the one who bought her. Waiting this last week was too much as it is.

I've waited long enough.

She wants a Dom and I want her. That's all that matters.

I watch as Alena shakes her head, although her eyes are hazed with curiosity. "I don't think an auction is what I'm looking for." *Good girl.*

I rise from my seat. Muting the microphones and buttoning my suit jacket. It's time for me to take over the tour and show Alena what she really needs.

CHAPTER 4

ALENA

The second play room is even more interesting than the first. It seems more private since it's smaller and there's only one of everything ... but there are so many items I'm not sure if multiple couples play together or not.

"How many people are usually in here?" I turn to Madam Lynn and ask. I love the idea of being at a Dom's mercy. But I'm not sure how I feel about other people watching. Especially at first, when I'm just learning. All of this is overwhelming to see in person.

I just don't think I could do it if strangers were watching. And the insecurity of it all is making me wonder if I can do this at all. I swallow thickly and wait for her to answer.

She's been patient and I really appreciate the tour. I didn't expect it. I also didn't expect it to be so empty.

"The play rooms are usually packed." My lips purse and my brow raises. Shit. I don't think I can handle that. I look around the room at the benches and sex swing and try to imagine being fucked mercilessly while tied down and having people watch. The first part heats my blood and makes desire stir low in my belly, but the second … it kills the fantasy for me.

I can't lie. I've been mused about this for a long time. More so recently since getting the email. I've touched myself to the thought of what it would've been like had I let Joshua dominate me like he wanted.

It caught me off guard back then. I kept thinking it was wrong and that he must've thought less of me. But now that I look back on it, he never treated me differently. He was just more aware of what he wanted. He shared his desires with me and fear kept me from submitting.

I wonder what it would have been like if I'd let him cuff me to the bed like he wanted to. What he would have done to me. I stifle my moan at the thought of him strapping me down and spreading my legs while I'm bound and helpless.

Madam Lynn's cough makes a blush stain my cheeks.

I turn and ignore the fact that my thoughts must've been obvious.

A frown pulls at my lips as I take in the room, remembering what we were just talking about. Coming here would be nothing like what I fantasize about. I'm not interested in an orgy or voyeurism. Whatever it is that they call it.

I was hopeful that this was going to fulfill my needs, but all this tour has done is fill me with regret. I wish I'd never ended things with Joshua. I let my fear push him away.

I bite the inside of my cheek.

"I wouldn't worry too much if I were you," Madam Lynn says, her seductive voice grabbing my attention and bringing me back to the present.

"Why's that?" I dare to ask.

She may be elegant and graceful, but Madam Lynn seems to be a woman of secrets. She has a look in her eyes and a manner of speaking that makes it obvious that she knows more than she's telling you. I'm not sure I like that, but considering her profession, it's admirable.

"I have a feeling you'll be spending most of your time in a private room." My shoulders relax slightly at the thought. Yes, I think I'd much prefer privacy.

I open my lips to ask to see the rooms, but my body freezes as my eyes catch sight of *him*. My heart, my blood, everything slows and heats to a nearly unbearable degree.

I blink a few times. Not believing he's here.

"Alena," Joshua steps into the room, proving that he's not a figment of my imagination. My entire body feels as though it's on fire.

Holy fuck!

Ten years ago he was a hot-as-fuck twenty year old. The years have aged him beautifully. His strong jawline and broad shoulders heighten the severity of his suit. Joshua has always radiated power, sex appeal and authority to me. But in this moment he is the epitome of dominance.

I almost take a step back as he walks closer to me, out of sheer instinct. But my lust for him has me frozen in place. I can hardly breathe as the images I was just conjuring flash before my eyes.

Prickles of want travel down my body, hardening my nipples.

Desire stirs in my core.

"I have more work to attend to," Madam Lynn says to no one in particular and not waiting for a response. she gracefully, yet quickly leaves me alone with Joshua.

This is not good.

As she closes the door behind her, the only thing I can think is that I am so fucked.

CHAPTER 5

JOSHUA

I excel at reading body language. And right now my Cherry is looking to bolt, but more than that, she's turned on. I have to resist the urge to smile. I want her. I want her badly. And it's obvious that she wants me too.

"Do you want to try it out?" I ask her as she tries to right herself. She still hasn't spoken and I can practically hear the questions on the tip of her tongue.

There's a spark between us, a recognition of desire and want. But our past is in the way and all I want is for it to move aside so I can take her like I'm meant to.

"Joshua," she finally says my name as I walk closer to her, standing at a safe distance, but close enough to talk easily.

"How are you Alena?"

She nods her head as her fingertips roll the hem of her dress nervously and she glances behind me at the door. Her cheeks are colored with a violent blush that looks beautiful on her.

"How did you-" she starts to ask, but she doesn't complete the thought.

It could be one of many questions.

How did I get here?

How did I know she was here?

I decide to lay it all out for her and let her choose what to do with it.

"I knew you were coming." I answer her. My heart races as her eyes widen. "In fact, I asked Madam Lynn to send you the invitation." I spot the large wing back chair and decide to take a seat. It will be less intimidating for her if I'm sitting.

Her lips part with a question and then slam shut. She blinks several times.

"I saw you a few weeks ago in the city and I couldn't believe you were here." I sit back in my chair, "I thought this may be better." I look her in the eyes and wait for a response. It may have been easier to stop her from leaving the coffee shop, to walk up to her at the elevator before she went to work. But that would have set the wrong precedent.

This is the relationship I want. And the one she needs.

Our needs have to be established. Without it, without her willing to give both of us what we need, this relationship will fail like it did before. This time I'm going to fight for it. I want her badly enough to convince her to give this a chance.

"I wanted to see you here. I wanted to offer you this." I gesture around the room.

She blinks several times and then a small breath leaves her and her eyes gaze with lust.

"You want this?" she asks me as though she's shocked by the truth. Her hands reach up to her collarbone and she looks at me with a raw vulnerability I've only seen in her eyes once. The night I first made her mine. All those years ago.

I nod my head once. "I want this with you."

She seems to come out of the lust filled haze and realize she's in a room with me, a man who she's hardly spoken to in years. But I'm still a man she once loved. A man who knew her better than anyone.

"You don't know me, Joshua," she starts to say although she's obviously bothered.

"I knew you well enough to know you'd want this." I know she's going to fight at first. She's not used to submitting, but I'll earn her trust, I'll show her it's worth it.

It's quiet for a moment as she takes in my confession. "Do you come here a lot?" she asks, changing the subject.

"I'm a partner in the business." Her mouth drops some and she looks around the room with more unease than before. Insecurity obvious on her face.

This is a turn for the worse and I don't understand why. I wasn't expecting it.

"What's wrong?" I ask.

She shakes her head and almost refuses to answer.

"What did I say?" although it's a question, there's a command in my tone.

She recognizes it and considers me for a moment. She may not know it, but this is just like any other submission. She can choose to trust that she can trust me and answer the question honestly, or she can blow it off or hide from it and run without giving me a chance. I wait with baited breath for her choice.

And finally she answers, "I just didn't realize you did this a lot."

It doesn't take me long to read between the lines. I stand and make my way over to her, holding her gaze. "Do you think I fuck a lot, Alena?" I walk close enough to touch her, but I don't yet. "You think this is a game for me and you don't want to be used and tossed aside?"

I know that's exactly what she's thinking. And why

wouldn't she? I work in the business of selling sex and she's going to want a commitment. She needs one.

"I don't." I tell her the truth. "This isn't about a quick fuck for me. I'm not a playboy. I didn't bring you here to toy with you. I want to see if this can work between us." I'm not ready to fall back into the deep relationship we had before. Not just yet. But I won't lie and say it's not something that's on the forefront of my mind. I want her as a submissive, but I can give her more than that.

I can give her everything, if only she'll let me.

"What do you want from me then?" she asks.

"I just want a chance. One I never got before." I take a step closer and gently brush my hand along her jaw, leaning in so I can whisper against her lips. "I want to show you how much you'd love it."

Her eyes close and I know she wants the same.

As she leans in, I pull away slightly. I need her to submit before I can give her anything else. She opens her eyes instantly at the loss of my touch. Her breathing is heavy and I know she's feeling insecure. I don't want that. But I need this first. It's too big a part of my life and my desires.

"Do you want to try it?" I ask and gesture to the bench behind her. It's a spanking bench made of plush leather and steel.

She turns to look behind her, pushing her soft

brunette hair out of her face.

"Right now?" she asks.

I nod my head once, "right now."

She may not be ready just yet. And I can wait, I can take it slow. But she's in need and I'm desperate to fulfill those needs.

"I don't know," she answers honestly.

"What don't you know about?"

"I don't think I trust myself right now," she smiles slightly letting out a small nervous laugh.

"You don't need to, just trust me." I look into her eyes and plead with her to give me this. To give *us* this. "I still want you Alena. I've never stopped wanting you."

She takes in a sharp breath, her hazel eyes heating with a lust that makes my dick harden.

"I want to," she whispers.

"What do you want?" I ask her.

"I want to... try it out." She barely gets the words out, but I heard them and it's all I need.

CHAPTER 6

ALENA

My heart is racing out of my chest.

What am I even doing?

I feel drunk from the pure seductive nature of this atmosphere. And from *him*. He always made me weak and he's doing it again right now.

Seeing him in this very room is a dream come true. But it's terrifying at same time. I feel like a naive girl all over again. I close my eyes and walk over to the bench. I want to do this. This is why I came here in the first place

This is for me. I need this.

I open my eyes at the thought and the look in Joshua's eyes pins me in place. It's predatory and full of lust. The desire evident on his face, but also... lower. His massive cock is hard and the outline of it is pressing against his suit pants.

I close my eyes again as he walks forward.

"Look at me, cherry." The command in his voice is hard and on edge. It's a tone he's only used with me once. I refused it then, but I won't now.

My eyes meet his piercing gaze.

"Yes?" I almost say sir. Simply because I know the language. I've done some research over the years. I'm familiar with this scenario and I want it. I want it desperately. Even if it's just for now.

Just this one time.

"I want you to lay down on your back on the bench." My body stiffens at his command. I'm not used to it. It's not what I anticipated either. I turn to look at the leather seat as my hands drift to the buttons on the top of my dress.

"I didn't tell you to undress," my eyes snap to Joshua's at his words.

"Yes, sir." The title slips out without my consent and the look on Joshua's face makes me want to say it again. And again and again. He's obviously pleased and that makes pride and motivation flow through my body. I hold onto them as I gently lay down on the bench. It's angled slightly, so my head is lower than my ass and it feels a bit awkward.

"That's my sweet cherry." Hearing the praise in Joshua's voice and the nickname he gave me so long ago fills me with warmth. *Cherry*. I loved it when he called me that. My thighs clench and my eyes close at the sweet memories of what we once had and what I walked away from all those years ago. But now I have a chance to have it back. I can give him what he's always needed. I know I can.

As I think the words, he brushes his hands up my thighs and loops his thumbs around my panties. I lift my hips as the thin fabric slides over my ass and he slowly pulls them down my legs. Goosebumps follow his path and my body ignites with an intense need for more.

"If you want me to stop, you'll say red. Do you understand?"

"Yes," I breathe the word.

I can't breathe as he takes them off me and tosses them onto the chair behind him. Oh fuck.

I swallow thickly and wait for his next command. My clit is throbbing with need and my nipples are hardened into peaks. I want him so much, it takes everything in me to just lay here and wait patiently for him.

His large hands grip the inside of my knees and spreads my legs wider. I grip the edge of the bench harder as he lowers himself closer to my bared pussy.

I'm fully exposed and feeling a mixture of desire and insecurity. It takes me back to our first time. It's just like that. All over again.

He pulls my dress up slightly over my hips and stares at my pussy with a hunger I've never seen on another man. My lips part with lust. I love the look in his eyes. I've missed it. I've missed *him*.

He kneels on the floor and grips my hips, moving my ass and tilting me so I'm where he wants me.

Oh, fuck. My neck arches and I want to watch and I want to run and hide all at the same time.

"Fuck, cherry," Joshua says as he trails a finger down my clit to the opening of my pussy. "You're soaking wet for me."

My clit throbs as he leans down and takes a languid lick. My neck arches and my mouth opens with the unexpected pleasure.

"Hold onto the bench," he says firmly and I look up at him and realize my hands are on his shoulders. I nod and quickly follow his command.

As soon as I do, he thrusts two thick fingers deep inside of me, making my back bow and sending spikes of pleasure shooting through my body. *Fuck, yes!*

My nipples harden and I instantly remember how he used to control my body. I know now why sex has never been the same. My body is a slave to his touch. *Only his.*

I writhe on the bench, but his firm grip on my hip keeps me pinned in place.

I can't help the moans spilling from my lips as he strokes my g-spot over and over again, making me climb higher and higher. Soft cries fill the room as my head thrashes.

So close. I'm so close.

As he sucks my clit into his mouth, massaging it with his tongue, my body ignites, coming alive with a pleasure that's unmatched. White spots flash before my eyes as I cry out my release.

My back arches and my hands reach up to grab his hair and push him closer to my pussy, but I'm quick to go back to the bench and obey him.

I grip onto the bench as hard as I can while he continues to suck my clit and fingerfuck every last bit of my orgasm out of me.

I gasp for air as my head falls to the side. Every inch of my body tingling with desire. I struggle to breathe and finally calm down as I hear a zipper. I look down my body and see Joshua's thick cock and my heart stops.

"Turn over cherry," his voice drips with desire as he gives me the command. He holds my hips, steadying me as I quickly do what he says and get into position even with the intensity of my orgasm still racing through my body in dim waves.

His deft fingers quickly strap the cuffs to my wrists and ankles and my heart races. I trust him. I do. I'd be lying if I said I wasn't partially scared, but I want this. I want to get over my fear. I want to *enjoy* this.

His hot breath on my ass makes me want more. He leaves a kiss on my right cheek as the trembling in my legs settles.

I can hardly breathe as he kisses up my body, pushing the dress above my waist, his fingers trailing softly up my body. A shiver runs down my body and I just want him right now. I don't want to wait.

His soft touches are torturous.

"I want you Cherry. Let me have you just like this, with nothing in-between us." His voice drips with lust and desperation as he gently sets his hands down on my hips. It makes me feel powerful. Even though I'm bound, it's my limits that he has to abide by and the knowledge makes me yearn for more. "It's what I've always wanted." He barely speaks the words.

I've been dreaming of this for so long.

"I know you want it to," he whispers into my ear. His hot breath sending shivers down my entire body.

I pull against the straps and moan, arching my neck to let his teeth graze down my neck. I give in to him like I want to. I trust him and I want him. It's now or never.

"Yes, Joshua. Please. Take me."

CHAPTER 7

JOSHUA

I've wanted this for too fucking long.

I line my dick up at her entrance and slam all the way in without hesitation. The bench tilts forward slightly, but it's bolted to the floor. I can fuck her as hard and fast as I want. And there's nothing to stop me from giving her just that.

She screams out a ragged cry of pleasure as I hammer into her tight pussy over and over again. I'm rough with her and ruthless, it's a hard fuck, but it's how I want her and I know she'll love it. The sounds of her pleasured moans and my hips slamming against her ass, fill my ears. I fucking love it.

I'm going to give her everything. I want her so consumed with pleasure that she can't think straight. I want her so sore tomorrow that she can't sit without remembering this.

She's mine.

I want her to know it with everything in her. I want to own this tight pussy. The thought makes me groan as she writhes under me as best she can although she's bound. It's a useless effort, but instinctual.

Fuck, she feels so good. Too good. I groan as I lean forward and nip along her shoulder, keeping up a relentless pace.

Her strangled cries of pleasure fuel me to push harder and deeper.

"Joshua!" she screams out my name as I push her limits. Yes! My name.

Her breathing is ragged and I love it. The sound fuels me onward.

She pulls at the leather cuffs on her wrists and I nip her earlobe, "stay still while I fuck you just how I want." If she pulls any more, the leather could rub against her wrists. I don't want that. Even more so, I want her to obey me. I want to give her a command that she can obey, even if it is against her instincts.

She bites down on her lip as I pound into her over and over. Fuck yes! She's perfect. She's trying so hard to stay still. Her head thrashes from side to side and she's holding her breath as her mouth opens into a perfect "O". She's so close.

"Scream for me as you cum on my dick, cherry." At my words, she cries out my name, her pussy spasming on my dick. Yes! My name! Because she's *mine*. I ride through her orgasm, hammering harder into her as I grip her hips. My blunt fingernails dig into the soft flesh and I piston my hips.

"Joshua!" she screams again and sucks in a sharp breath and it only fuels me to go faster, to take her over the edge again. I want to give her everything.

I need to. This is my one chance to have her and show her how good this is going to be. How easy it is and how much she'll enjoy it.

I keep fucking her, over and over with hard, fast strokes, taking her to the edge.

My balls draw up and a cool tingling sensation grows at the base of my spine. Fuck, I'm going to cum. She's so tight and so good, I can't fucking hold it any longer.

"Cum for me again," I tell her with my eyes firmly on her gorgeous face as my hand reaches between the bench and I gently pinch her clit.

Her face scrunches and her body tenses as her orgasm rips through her body. She pulls instinctually at the binds, but she's quick to correct the behavior. Fuck, she's so good. Knowing that even as she's overwhelmed with pleasure, she's still trying to obey me, makes me lose it.

I bury myself to the hilt and pump short, shallow thrusts until we're both spent and left panting with our combined cum leaking onto her thighs.

My body is still humming with the afterglow of my release as I grab a few tissues from beneath the bench and catch my breath. I tuck myself in, watching as her legs stop trembling and the effects of her orgasm dims.

She was perfect. Everything I've dreamed of having in a submissive. From the moment she decided to walk to the bench and give this a real try, she gave herself completely.

I kiss the small of her back as I wipe the cum from between her thighs and then unbuckle the straps on her ankles. Her wrists are next and she immediately sits.

I pick her up in my arms and she leans into me, her body still trembling. I lean back and sooth her, running my hand down her back and kissing her hair. She's so beautiful. The years have only made her more of a woman. After a moment she moves from my lap, not looking me in the eyes. I don't like it. Aftercare is important, but I let her get up and move to the chair where her panties are.

I regret letting her get up when I see the look in her

eyes. She's on edge and nervous. She's thinking too much. Worrying about what's going to happen.

If she was my sub she wouldn't have a worry in the world. And I want her to be just that.

She leans down and pulls her panties on and up her lush thighs without looking at me.

I bet she's wondering what this meant to me and if it's over.

I don't want her to wonder; I don't want her to think about anything at all but pleasing me. After all, I'm doing the same.

"I have a Christmas dinner tomorrow to attend for a client." The words escape my lips before I can think. Her forehead pinches and she's unsure why I'm even bringing it up. "I want you to come with me."

She stares at me wide-eyed and doesn't answer.

"A submissive doesn't question the commands." I pick my suit jacket up off the floor and wait for her response. "You know what to say Alena."

I wait with baited breath. This is about more than sex for me. And I damn well know the same is true for her. She just needs to give in.

"You came in here for a reason cherry." Her eyes dart to mine. "Let me give you what you need."

Her lips part with uncertainty.

"I want you. As submissive and more. I want you to

be mine."

Her eyes focus on my lips and I know I have her. If nothing else, she loves my touch. But I know there's more to it than that. You don't hold on to this desire and these feelings if there isn't *more* to it.

"Just say yes, Cherry. Let me collar you, like you really want me to."

She says the next words in the sweetest voice I've ever heard, "collar me, Joshua. I'm ready."

Epilogue

Alena

I twist my hands and struggle to move. I've been waiting here on the bed, tied down by my wrists and ankles for at least twenty minutes. In the six months that we've dated, Joshua has never made me wait this long.

I'm naked and horny and so ready for him to take me. But I lay here quietly and wait. I know he's going to come in and give me exactly what I need. And I trust him to do just that.

A small smile plays at my lips.

The only thing I really need is him. I sigh with contentment, feeling warm and safe. He's my security in life. I feel complete with him. I didn't even realize how much I was missing from life until he showed me.

My eyes slowly open and my pussy clenches as I hear the door creak open.

My chest flushes and heat travels to my cheeks. I'm spread and naked and I know he's seeing everything. But that's the way he wants me.

"Cherry, you're so damn patient," he says from behind me as he walks into the bedroom.

"For you," I answer with a smirk. Really, he's the patient one. It took me ten years to accept that I wanted this. Ten years for me to let him show me how much I'd love it.

The bed groans as he crawls closer to me. He's hiding something in his hand and excitement courses through me at the thought of what it could be.

"I got you a present," he says seductively. I smile broadly and let my teeth sink into my bottom lip to try to conceal my elation.

Ever since our second night together, he brings me little gifts while I'm tied up. That second night was Christmas Eve and he gave me a collar. It's beautiful and I love it. I wear the necklace, another gift from Joshua, outside of Club X, but inside and in the bedroom, I proudly wear my collar.

"What is it?" I ask.

"Uh uh, close your eyes." I smile sweetly at him, my

eyes darting from his handsome face to his closed hand.

I close my eyes and wait patiently. My blood heats and my breath stills as he leans over and slips a cold metal ring onto my ring finger. *Oh my god.*

"Marry me Cherry." Joshua says in a voice that has a hint of insecurity.

I keep my eyes closed. Still in disbelief.

"Say yes." He gives me another command.

I slowly open my eyes and stare back at him.

"You're mine, Alena. And I want you forever and for everyone to know it."

Tears prick my eyes and I nod my head. "I love you," I say as he bends down, kissing me sweetly. He breaks our kiss and says in the hot air between us, "you need to say yes."

"Yes," I whisper. He takes my lips with his and groans into my kiss. I have to pull away and struggle against the damn binds pinning me down. I just want to hold him.

A rough chuckle rises up his chest as he reaches over and unties my wrists and then my ankles.

It's then that I get a good look at the sparkling ring on my finger. It's a beautiful cushion cut with perfect clarity and at least three carats. I stare at it in awe.

"I had to tie you down and make sure you'd say yes."

I shake my head, my shoulders shuddering with a small laugh, "you had to know I'd say yes." I've never wanted anything more than this. My life feels truly complete. "You collared me for Christmas," I jokingly say back to him.

He shakes his head and looks at the gorgeous engagement ring on my finger. "For life my cherry."

Stolen Mistletoe Kisses

CHAPTER 1

VINNY

The brightly colored mouse face on the plastic phone in my hands stares back at me. I remember this toy, with its primary colors of red, yellow, and blue, and the loud noises the buttons make. I can't pull the little phone out, but I know there's a thin red cord that's connected so little tykes can drag it along the floor. I huff a small laugh.

Same damn toy I had as a toddler, twenty-five years later.

Some things never change.

I set the box back on the shelf and look over to my left. This aisle in the toy store lines up with the door to the back room, which in turn leads to the manager's office. That's right where I need to go. I'm just waiting on the perfect moment to slip into the back and grab the spare key. The manager slipped out already; he clocked out early even though the store's still open. I don't blame him, since it's dead. In this small town, everyone's done their shopping early for Christmas.

The owner and him are the only two with the keys to the registers, but now they're both gone and won't be back till after Christmas, and I know the keys are back there somewhere.

The old lady behind me finally tosses something into her cart, making a small racket and a squeak. I turn to look over my shoulder and watch as she pushes her cart away. I take the chance, looking to my right and left as I make my way to the "employees only" door and confidently open it.

As though I belong back here.

My heart's racing, and adrenaline is pumping through my veins. This isn't the first time I've done something like this. It's been years since I've jacked a car or stolen anything. Back then I was a thief for hire. I'm not proud of it. But now I stay on the right side of the law. I peek into the break room and see it's empty. Stockroom is next and there's a girl bending at the waist digging in a box, muttering about how the color of the dress on the doll isn't gonna matter. I keep walking until I find the door with the Manager's Office plate on it.

Bingo.

I test the knob and it doesn't budge. But that's alright. I may be a reformed man, but I still remember how to pick a lock. I stare at the door for a moment, then look back to the storefront at the end of the hallway as I shove a bent paperclip in the lock.

This isn't about stealing for me. It's about doing the right thing. Maybe it's the wrong way of going about it, but it's the only way I know.

The lock clicks and I'm quick to open the door, walking in as swiftly and quietly as possible and shut it behind me with a soft low *snick*. My heart pounds, and I can hear the blood rushing in my ears.

I stalk to his desk and check there first. I need the keys to the register. I need that cash. I know this old toy shop doesn't have a safe. All the money's stored in the registers, and I need that fucking key.

It's not on the desk. I open one drawer after another, sifting through all the paperwork and looking under the stapler and pens.

Where the fuck is it? I know he didn't take it with him. He's got the key to the entrance doors though and I wasn't able to lift that like I would have liked. My eyes look up and hone in on something shining on the bookshelf filled with binders.

A smile crawls across my face.

The tiny key that's been a pain in my ass the last week to get is hanging on a keychain, and I don't hesitate to grab it. Finally. The last piece falls into place. I shove it in my pocket, knowing I'm one step closer to completing this task. Nothing's going to stop me.

I put my ear to the door and listen for anyone coming. I don't hear anything, so I open it slowly and peek out.

The chick who was digging in the box is walking toward the door leading out to the rest of the store with her back to me. She's empty-handed and muttering to herself with her hands balled into little fists. She huffs a deep breath like she's getting ready to go to war over this doll. I shut the door and wait a moment, listening for the telltale sound of the heavy door opening and then shutting. *Click.*

Once the coast is clear, I sneak another look and make sure.

No one's there. My throat feels dry and my face is heated, knowing I need to make a clean getaway out of here and back into the store.

I lock the manager's office door behind me and make a beeline for my escape. As soon as I'm back to the customer area, I feel a slight sense of relief. But I need to get the fuck out of here. One rule I always lived by back in the day, you never stick around to find out if someone saw you.

There's no security in this place though. I know that for a fact.

If there were, I wouldn't have to do this. They would've caught that bastard in the act, and it wouldn't be left up to me to get justice.

I walk quickly toward the exit, through a few aisles of toy trucks and stacking blocks, but I stop before walking through the large automated glass doors.

Cary Ann's standing at the register. Sweet Cary. The sight of her makes me stop before I can leave.

I've known her most of my life since we grew up together in this small town, but scoping this place out has made me see her in a new light. It's been years since I really *looked* at her. And now I can't stop. She's not the little girl who'd fawn over me on the school sidewalks. She's a woman now.

Her tight, faded jeans fit her figure just right and make my dick hard as a fucking rock. They leave nothing to the imagination, and I can just picture how the curve of her ass would feel in my hands. I don't know how it's possible that I ever looked at her with anything other than lust; she's fucking gorgeous.

Her white tanktop is low enough that a bit of cleavage is showing, but the red cardigan she has partially buttoned up over it makes her look a bit more modest. I crave more. I wanna see more of that sun-kissed skin. Every inch.

She's always popping that bubble gum, blowing big, round, cherry-red bubbles at the checkout counter. *Pop!*

It's like she knows she's tempting me with her sweet innocent glances. I don't even know what she's still doing here; she's better than this.

She's got her degree in social work, and I know she doesn't want to work here at the toy store forever. This was a side job for money while she was at the university. She shouldn't be here.

I clear my throat as the front doors open and an older lady walks out, clutching her cardigan.

Cary's a distraction. And she's sure as fuck too good for a man like me.

I thought she'd be gone by now. In the weeks I've been staking this place out, I never thought she'd still be here. But Christmas is around the corner, and she's not showing any signs of leaving or even putting in her notice.

That's a big fucking problem for me. I'm stealing every fucking dime in this place on Christmas Eve. She can't be here, but she's scheduled to be the one closing. All alone, too. I can't pull a gun out and point it at my cherry. The thought of putting fear into those innocent baby blues breaks my heart.

But I'm not the villain here; Jimmy Morose, the owner, is a greedy thief. He's practically the fucking Grinch. All the money that was supposed to go to the orphanage, he's already stolen. I'm getting it back though, and that means emptying these tills at midnight on Christmas Eve. It's the perfect time, right when the annual Christmas Eve parade will be happening and the police will all be there on the other side of town. It's then, or never.

But Cherry's going to be here... A grin slips into place. I could just steal her, too.

CHAPTER 2

CARY ANN

He's here again, and he still hasn't bought a damn thing. Not that a man like him looks like he needs anything in this toy store. I think he's just coming to check me out. Or at least I thought he was. But he hasn't said a damn word to me. Maybe I'm just vain or getting carried away with the thoughts I used to have of him.

Vinny's a bad boy... or bad *man*, I should say.

I knew him growing up, and lusted after his I-don't-give-a-fuck attitude. He wore his leather jacket and rode that motorcycle everywhere. I wanted to be on the back of that bike. I wanted him to take me away. I shake off the thoughts and swallow down my childhood fantasies.

I was just a silly little girl. My parents would never have allowed it, and he was a few years older anyway. He wasn't interested in a girl like me. Besides, I'm better for it now. I have my degree in social work, and I've already nailed down the job of my dreams. I'm going to be making the world a better place.

I'm not saying Vinny would've held me back, but I'm damn proud that I was able to focus on school and my career.

And to be wise enough to know what's been going on around here.

Now Vinny's back, and he's tempting me. But judging by the puppy dog look on his face, I'm tempting him just as much.

My heart beats just a little faster, and my blood heats with lust. *Pop!* I blow out a bubble and hide my smile when I see him shake his head and smirk at me. My cheeks heat with a blush as I lower my head out of shyness and ring up the remote control car for the mom that's checking out.

"But I want it!" her little boy screams from the seat in his cart, and his loud shriek brings me back to the present.

He's a cute little guy in a snowman sweatshirt, jeans and little boots that look like they could take on a blizzard. But his high-pitched yells and him kicking the cart are driving me crazy. And giving me a headache.

"You want to just hand it to him, or do you want it in a bag?" I ask the mom. I feel bad that she's got two kids out here this late at night. That's gotta be a handful and even worse since they're obviously tired. She looks worn the fuck out. Her hair's pulled back into a ponytail and the little infant in her arms is trying to yank on her earring, which is a miniature Christmas ornament. I wince. That looks like it hurts.

The woman leans her head down so her baby isn't tugging on the earring, seething through her clenched teeth; the pain is evident on her face as she pries the little fingers off of the dangling jewelry. The little girl squeals with delight in her mama's arms and the woman gives the baby a small smile, but switches her to the other hip.

I don't know what good that's gonna do, since the little girl just focuses on that side's earring now.

"No thanks, can you bag it please?" she answers with a forced smile and leans forward to talk to the boy in the cart. "You have to wait, little man." Good for her for at least holding it together.

The boy comically crosses his arms across his chest with a pout, and I have to stifle my laughter as I ring her up.

Once she's done, the store's basically empty. And it's only a few minutes before close. Thank God. I'm spent. I'm ready to get out of here and grateful that so many people are shopping online. I yawn and cover my mouth, then look back to where Vinny was standing. He's gone, and the sight of the empty aisle makes a frown touch my lips. I don't know why, but I just want him to say hi. To just acknowledge my presence. He never did growing up, but I never talked to him either. I didn't have the courage back then. Now though... I need to suck it up and let him know I'm interested. I can do that. I should've already.

He's been in here three times this week, and he's never bought a damn thing. The knowledge makes my stomach twist in knots.

He's up to no good. I hate that I think that. That's what everyone said when he was growing up. They pretend like they don't know why he ended up doing shady things when they never even gave him a chance at anything else. From what I know, he's a good man now. He's got his life together. And I hate that I think anything negative about him at all. But why the hell does he keep coming in here?

I hated the way the parents and teachers all talked about him when we were younger, yet I find myself thinking he's gotta be up to something.

Or maybe I'm just projecting my own actions onto his behavior. My blood cools at the thought, but I can't focus on that right now.

I smile as I ring up the last two customers in the entire place. At least there aren't any more kids in here yelling. I've taken so much Advil the past week that I should really consider buying stock in them.

I'm leaving soon though; this job isn't forever. I just need to stay until Christmas. I have to. I need to be here and make sure everything goes the way it's supposed to on Christmas Eve.

With the store finally empty, I go through the daily closing checklist and take a peek down one aisle. It's a fucking disaster.

Cindy's crouched down, picking up dolls off the floor and shoving them back into place on the shelf. "I bet it was that little brat," she says under her breath when she sees me. I have to press my lips together and hide my grin. She's had a really hard day and given the fact that she only stayed on later because the manager ducked out early, I can see why she's pissed.

"I can take these if you wanna line up aisle three?" I ask her. I know she prefers the larger toys. They're mostly in boxes and easier to straighten out.

She sighs and looks up at me, shoving her blonde hair out of her face. "It doesn't matter really. I'm just tired and ready to go home." She looks fucking exhausted.

"Go ahead," I say with a shrug, "I got this." I don't

mind taking a little more work anyway. *Besides, it'll give me a chance to get things ready for Christmas Eve.* The thought makes my skin prickle with nerves.

"You are a saint, Cary." She rises slowly and stretches out before giving me an unexpected hug.

"Thank you," she says and then doesn't look back as she heads out the front doors to the parking lot. For this town, nine o'clock is late for any place to be open. But for the holiday season it's worth it to be open another three hours on Sunday. At least that's what Morose thinks, but he's a liar, a thief, and an asshole. Judging by the lack of business, you can add dumbass to that list.

I have to straighten two more rows, all the while wondering if I'm going to be able to go through with my plan, and then I turn out the lights and lock the doors. I've been sick over this. I can't stand it, and I want to make things right.

But I'm struggling with what I need to do. I'm not a criminal. And what I'm planning on doing is a crime. I run my hand over my face, feeling torn and exhausted as I walk to the parking lot. It's late, and the street lights are dim. My heels click on the pavement, and my keys rattle in my hand. I look at the ground as I carefully watch my step, avoiding the potholes in the parking lot that Jimmy Morose hasn't bothered to get fixed yet. The only sounds I hear are my heels, and I think I'm alone, but when I lift my head, I stop in my tracks.

Vinny.

He's leaning against my car, his motorcycle parked behind him.

CHAPTER 3

VINNY

I *can at least get her number*, I think as I walk out of the store. Take her on a date. Maybe then I can convince her to quit. Or better yet, wear her out and make her pussy so sore she won't be able to work on Christmas Eve.

The thought makes me smile as I take out my cell and text Toni. I let him know it's all set for Christmas Eve and then sit on my bike watching the little boy across the parking lot say "please" over and over again to the mom who looks like she's gonna snap any minute. She's got a cart full of toys by her trunk, a little boy kicking the cart for enjoyment while begging for something, and the baby in her arms is throwing a fit.

Last-minute shopping doesn't look like it's treating her well.

"You need a hand with that?" I ask her, walking away from my bike and over to her minivan. The night air is crisp, and my boots smack against the pavement.

"Please," she says as she looks up at me, but it doesn't last long as her infant arches her back and lets out a shrill cry. "I thought they'd sleep," she says with desperation cracking her voice. Poor mama. I feel bad for her as I reach in the cart and grab a few of the bags in each hand.

She opens the trunk and then the side door before placing her keys back in her purse. "My husband had to work late," she starts explaining, as if she owes me that, but she doesn't. I get it. Sometimes we do shit we wish we didn't have to. "And he was supposed to do the shopping for his side of the family, and he never did." She talks while plugging her little one into the carseat. I can faintly hear the clicking of the buckles.

The rustling from a plastic bag makes me look up, and I catch her little boy trying to grab one of the bags.

She shuts the door and comes around the rear of the van with her hands on her hips. "Jaxon!" she yells out. The little boy looks up with big wide eyes and his lips in a perfect "O." He's been caught red-handed. And he knows it. The look of fear is evident in his eyes and the entire thing makes me chuckle, but I turn away so he doesn't think this is funny. Little rascal.

She snatches him out of the cart and moves to the other side of the van to put him in his carseat. He can't be any older than three. He's silent the entire time and looks stiff, like he knows he's in trouble. At least he's not throwing a fit.

I load the last few bags in and shut her trunk with a loud clunk and start rolling the cart back over a few parking spots to the cart corral to join the rest of them.

I look back over my shoulder as I hear the door close.

"Thank you," the woman says with a look of sincerity.

"No problem," I answer back, giving her a little wave as I shove the cart into the others.

"Merry Christmas," she says, grabbing the keys from her purse and walking to the driver's door, her boots smacking on the pavement. As she opens the door, I can hear her little girl wailing. I cringe out of instinct.

"Merry Christmas," I say, but I don't bother raising my voice since I doubt she can hear me.

I haven't had many people tell me that this season. *Merry Christmas.* I'm not used to hearing it anyway. Same with the rest of the holidays.

I grew up alone, and I'm fine with that. But it's nice to hear holiday greetings occasionally. I can't deny that. The older I get, the more I realize how much I want it.

I click my phone to check the time, shaking off the

unwelcome feelings. Cary Ann's gotta be closing up soon, so I might as well wait for my cherry.

I tap the phone against my jeans, staring at the building. This is bad news. I shouldn't even be going after her, but I *want* her. Something about her is calling to me. I can't justify it. In fact, this can only complicate things. But still I lie to myself.

I can convince her to stay away. I can keep her out of danger by getting close to her.

That's enough to slip a smile across my face as I head on over to my bike and take a seat while I wait for her.

I get lost in my emails on my phone. Since I've been distracted with this heist, I've fallen behind on orders for my custom-made choppers. But I'm calling the delay a holiday break, and my customers don't seem to mind. They don't have much of a choice either. There's a reason they come to me. No one can build choppers like I can. If I'd known all those years ago that I could make good money doing this, I never would've gone down the path I did. I shove down the regret. The past is in the past, and I've moved on.

I look up as a sweet little thing strolls out of the store and walks straight to a beat-up, faded white Honda in the parking lot. It's not my girl, it's the chick who was getting all wound up in the back room. I smile to myself remembering how pissed off she was, and return to my phone, wondering if the customer even got the doll.

I stop what I'm doing when I feel her eyes on me. For a moment, I freeze. *Fuck.* I shouldn't be lingering out front. What if it seems suspicious? How fucking ironic would it be if I got caught because I was waiting for her? Something that has nothing to do with this shit I have planned.

The girl starts her car and sits there a minute, looking at me in her rearview before driving away. She looks back at me again when she gets to the stop sign and then pulls off as I meet her gaze.

No, that's not gonna happen. My cherry will tell them I was just waiting on her. I know she will. Yeah, that's just one more reason to pursue her. Now she's my alibi.

Every time I was here, it was just to see her sweet ass and work up the courage to ask her out.

I grunt a laugh, seeing as how that's sorta what happened, too. I'd feel pathetic over the thought if I really stopped to think about how this girl's got me twisted up in knots, but I stop that thought in its tracks.

It's the way she looks at me. I'm affecting her just as much and the moment she steps out of that store, I know I'm not gonna have any problems making her mine. As if accepting the challenge, she slips out of the building and locks the doors behind her.

I think about how easy it'd be to just lift them off of her. I could do that. Maybe I should. If we had the keys, it wouldn't have to be a stick-up; without them we'd be left to break a window, and that would trigger the alarm. That's something we don't want. The thought lingers in my mind, but it's quickly replaced by the sight of her lush ass in those jeans.

Damn, I can't wait to get her writhing underneath me. My dick is rock hard as her hips sway and she strolls toward her car. I get off my bike and wait for her. She seems lost in thought as I lean against her passenger side door. She doesn't even see me at all. She should be paying attention out here alone at night.

Fuck, my dick twitches in my jeans. We could fuck right here and right now, and no one would ever know. This town is old and small. Everyone's home this late at night. And this shopping strip is mostly vacant and on the edge of town. We could get away with it.

My cherry's not that kind of girl though, I know she's not. She's not gonna be giving it up that fucking easy. And I'm fine with waiting. For a night, anyway. And then I'll make sure she warms up to me.

She finally looks up, and her eyes go wide as she takes me in and stops walking in her tracks. I give her a cocky smirk and nod my head. "You finally got off?"

She blushes at my words, and it's only then that

I realize the double meaning. My sweet cherry has a dirty mind.

"Vinny, right?" she asks, swinging the keys in her hand and walking up to me full of confidence with a playful smile gracing her lips.

Fuck, I love that about her. Her confidence. I know she's a shy girl at heart, but she's got a way of putting it all out there for me. I fucking love that.

"Cary Ann," I reply and nod my head as I let my eyes roam down her tight body. I want her to see me appreciating her curves. It's pretty fucking cold out here, and her coat's hiding a lot of her body, but the plump part of her breasts is peeking up and flushed with the chill of the December night.

"What are you doing out here?" she asks as she moves around to her side of the car and I follow behind. She opens up the door and leans against it, giving me a generous view of her ass and taunting me. I adjust my dick real quick while she's not looking, and she actually wiggles her ass some. She definitely teasing me.

"Oh, don't tempt me," I warn her as she puts the key in the ignition and starts her car. It's not that cold that she's gotta warm her car up. It never gets that cold this far south, but I do appreciate the view.

She blushes and looks over her shoulder. "Oh yeah?" she says before sinking her teeth into her bottom lip. I wasn't actually considering fucking her against her car, but if she keeps this up that's exactly what's going to happen.

"Come on, Cherry," I say and lower my voice, "I'm trying to be good for you."

She straightens herself as I walk closer to her. She looks up at me, batting those thick lashes as she says, "I heard you were bad."

I stiffen at her confession, but she leans in and whispers, "That's what I like about you." Her hot breath tickles my neck as the sweet words touch my ear, and a playful smile spreads on my lips.

She pulls back with her eyes sparkling, and lust clearly present.

"Good. 'Cause I wanna take you out and show you a good time." I get right to the point before I do end up crushing her body against this car and giving us both what we want.

Her smile widens, and that shy side about her comes through as she brushes her hair out of her face and tucks it behind her ear. "I'd like that." A blush brightens her cheeks. "I was wondering when you were gonna ask me."

My brow pinches in confusion.

She gestures to the store and explains, "You kept coming in, but you never said anything." I swallow my nerves and smile back at her, but internally I feel like I'm suffocating. It's not good that she noticed, but this is the perfect cover-up.

I shrug it off and say, "I was just waiting till it felt right."

We both turn to face the entrance to the parking lot as the white Honda from earlier drives through and comes straight for us. The girl from earlier takes a look at me and then says, "Cary, you doing alright?"

Cary laughs a little, walking to her friend and bending over to lean into the window as she replies, "I'm fine, Cindy. Just getting asked out on a date," she says, staring at me over her shoulder and clearly looking pleased. It's a little irritating to be interrupted, but I have to admit it's a nice thing for her friend to do. I can't say that I blame her; I was looking a little sketchy earlier. The suspicious gaze she was giving me with narrow eyes turns into a surprised and somewhat excited look.

"Did you really drive all the way back here to check on me?" Cary asks with a hint of disbelief.

Cindy rolls her eyes and shrugs before saying, "Sue me for being a good friend and caring about your ass." She grins at Cary and gives me a quick wave. "Alrighty then, I'll leave you two to it."

A rough chuckle rises up my chest as she pulls away and my cherry walks back to me slowly.

"So, tomorrow night?" I ask her as the back lights from the Honda fade in the distance down the street, feeling cocky. My dick's already hardening at the thought of getting her under me.

"That's the night before Christmas Eve; I have a family dinner." Oh, yeah. I forgot for a moment. It's not like I have anything going on, but most people do.

She's looking all sorts of disappointed, like it really hurt her to tell me no. "Sorry. We decorate the tree. It's a family tradition."

"That makes sense." I don't have family traditions. You need a family in order to have them. Yet another difference, another reason we shouldn't be together. The thought takes me back.

I'm not planning a future with my cherry. I struggle for a moment to remember why I'm out here with her. Why I waited with the intention of seeing her and planning our little date. I need to get her out of the store on Christmas Eve. Yeah, that's the reason. I'm a fucking liar. I just wanna get her under me.

She shrugs and says, "It's early, and my mom's usually tipsy and passed out by eight." She sways from side to side, shrugging. "I can skip out. Meet you a little later?" Her voice practically purrs on the last line.

"Fuck, yeah. It's a date."

CHAPTER 4

CARY ANN

This is stupid. I have butterflies and I'm nervous and I feel so childish, but thinking about Vinny reminds me how I used to feel about him. I'd walk back home from school while he drove away on his motorcycle, just dreaming about being on the back, my arms around his waist. Imagining how he'd kiss me outside of school. I huff a small laugh and bring my beer to my lips.

Times have changed, but I can't help feeling the nerves from way back then.

I watch as a customer rings the little bells scattered along the holly on the bar. That, along with Christmas music, is really making it feel like the holidays. The holly also has fake snow on it, and there's a snowman spray-painted with more fake snow on the front window of the bar, too.

It's cute, but some asshole is running his finger through it and pissing off the bartender, who I'm guessing is the one who made the artwork. I look straight ahead and just ignore him. The guy's drunk, and the bartender doesn't do anything but shake his head, then continues wiping down the glasses. I imagine he's gotta spray-paint a new snowman every night.

"No mistletoe?" I jump a little in my seat and almost spill my beer when I hear his voice. *Vinny.*

I give Vinny a small smile and set my beer down, trying to remember what he asked as my heartbeat calms back down. His voice is so deep and rough that it makes desire stir in my belly.

My cheeks flush when I finally realize what he said. *Mistletoe.* I'm a strong, confident woman, but this man brings out a shy side of me that I haven't felt in years.

I start picking at the label on my beer bottle and shake my head with my teeth sunk into my bottom lip. "Not here," I whisper in the sexiest voice I can.

I dressed the part tonight, wearing a deep red dress that clings to my figure. I know it's tight and a bit provocative for this bar, but I want to look good for him. I want to show off this feminine side of me. I want to show him that I'm a woman now, and that I want exactly what he has to offer.

Part of me feels self-conscious, while another part of me feels slutty. But I don't care. I want him, and I'm not letting him go without trying.

He takes a seat at the bar, looking up at the college football game on the TV behind the bar as he slides off his leather jacket. All he's wearing underneath is a clean crisp t-shirt that hugs his broad shoulders tightly, and a pair of faded blue jeans. Fuck, even in casual clothes he looks like a million bucks.

Suddenly the expensive dress I wore makes me feel cheap. I stop picking at the stupid label on the bottle and finally take another swig.

"You look beautiful, Cherry," he says in a deep low voice that's somehow directly connected to my clit. I turn to look at him when I feel those baby blue eyes on me.

I'm not letting him go without making it damn well obvious what I want tonight.

He's my Christmas present to myself. If that makes me a ho, then I'll ho ho ho myself right to his bedroom. Definitely his, since I'm still at my parents' house until I start my new job. I visibly cringe at the thought.

Vinny laughs, and then orders a beer. "What, you don't like my nickname for you?" he asks me.

I let out a small laugh and smile, feeling the light

buzz of the beer and accepting another as the bartender slides the glass bottles toward us on the bar.

"I like your nickname for me. It sounds dirty when you say it," I confess and blush violently at my own words and silently blame it on the alcohol.

He cocks a brow at me and leans in as he asks, "Is that so, Cary Ann?" His hot breath lingers on my neck and creates a shiver that slowly runs down my body, hardening my nipples. His lips barely touch the shell of my ear as he huskily says, "I didn't know you were a dirty girl... Cherry."

I laugh it off even though I'm all hot and bothered. I want him to know that I want him, but I'm not going to make it *too* easy for him.

"So what are your plans for Christmas Eve?" I ask casually, and then I remember my own plans. All the desire leaves me, and my mouth goes dry. I grip my beer a little harder. My heart races in my chest. I have to work, but more importantly, I need to make sure everything goes smoothly.

I need to stop the video camera footage first. My blood heats with anxiety. I'm not letting Morose do this again. That orphanage matters to me, and I know for a fact last year he did the same thing. The donations are truly needed, and that greedy fucker took it all. I saw the check he wrote to himself. I didn't want to believe it, but when I asked Mrs. Pilcavage if the check went through and she said she hadn't gotten it, my heart truly broke. She's an older lady and she believes what he tells her. It's so wrong. I can't stand it. I'm going to do the right thing, even if it costs me everything.

"Not much," Vinny says and shrugs and then seems to stare off at the television for a moment. I have to get my shit together. I take a deep breath, trying to calm myself down.

I've never done anything like this, but I'm not going to let anything stand in my way of making sure I take every cent from the registers and giving it to the orphanage where it rightfully belongs.

And on top of that, I have proof of what Morose did so he goes to jail for being the thief he is. But I'm not waiting on the law. I'm making sure those kids have the best Christmas they've ever had.

The last thought fills me with conviction.

Anger courses through my blood, but the sight of Vinny staring back at me changes it to something else. Something stronger, something hotter that I can't deny.

This shit is for me to worry about tomorrow night. Everything's going to go down perfectly. So tonight I'm going to relax. With *him*.

"So nothing for Christmas Eve then?" I ask casually and then set the bottle down on the bar. I remember he's from the orphanage, and my heart hurts a little. He grew up there for a few years before his aunt finally took him in. I can't believe I forgot. I take another drink to stop all the emotions from creeping up on me.

I have to change the subject, fast. "You looking forward to anything for Christmas?" I ask him.

He looks above me at the holly and asks again, "Mistletoe?"

I laugh a little, making my shoulders shake some.

"How about a kiss then?" he finally asks me, leaning in.

I smile shyly at him, but I'm not shy about this kiss. I'm more than happy to give it to him. I want *more* though.

I lean in slightly and he goes for it, but I put my finger to his lips and stop him. His eyes slowly open and they narrow at me, as if daring me to deny him. The hidden threat lying there in his baby blues ignites that desire full force.

"I'm gonna need you to take me home first," I whisper against his lips.

I gasp at the heat that blazes in his eyes. "That can be arranged, Cherry," he says. "Finish your beer, and then you're coming home with me."

CHAPTER 5

VINNY

I can't rip this dress off of her fast enough.

Her fingers kept inching closer and closer to my dick while I drove her back here. We left her car at the bar and she rode with me on the back of my bike, her warmth on my back and her breasts pressed against me. I was already hard just feeling her curves, but then those hands...

My cherry is a naughty girl, and I fucking love it.

Her nails gently scratched at the waistline of my jeans until the tips of her fingers were buried inside.

"Cherry," I admonished her as we pulled up to a red light. But all she did was lean forward, taking my lips with hers and moaning into my mouth.

Fuck, my dick twitches thinking about how I wanted to take her right then and there.

I slam her back against the wall of my foyer, kicking the front door shut behind me and struggling to get these fucking clothes off. I should get a damn medal for waiting until I got her home behind closed doors.

Her lips press to mine, molding to my easy pressure as I slip my tongue into her hot mouth. She kisses me with a passion I've never had with anyone else as my hands roam her body.

I grip her ass in my hands and pull her up to me, her legs wrapping around my hips like a good girl.

Fuck, if I'd known how much she wanted me, I would've skipped the bar entirely. I pick her up and walk to my bedroom. No shame, and no fucks given. We're both adults with needs, and I'm ready to strip her down and relieve all this sexual tension between us. My hand's up her dress and caressing her smooth skin, while her nails dig into my shoulders and her other hand grips my hair.

"Vinny," she moans my name. I take the break in our kiss to graze my teeth down her neck and leave open-mouth kisses all along the exposed skin. As the front of my legs hit the bed frame, I throw her ass down on it and smile when she lets out a playful squeal.

I'm quick to take off my shirt and then reach over for

the light on the nightstand. I slowly unbuckle my jeans and look back at my sweet cherry on the bed.

She's looking all kinds of hot and bothered, and a little shy, too.

She's still wearing her dress although her heels are gone, lost somewhere between the foyer and the bedroom.

"Take that off, Cherry," I say beneath my breath, looking at her with obvious hunger in my eyes.

She looks to the light switch and visibly swallows. "Can we turn the lights off?" she asks softly. Her confident energy is gone, and her insecurity is coming through. A part of me wants to give in and let her have whatever she wants, just grateful that a girl like Cherry wants to be with a man like me. But that's not happening. I wanna see her.

"No," I shake my head, holding her gaze. Her expression falls slightly and I shove my pants down and stalk over to her, buck naked. The bed groans as I crawl closer to her, my dick hard and ready. "I wanna watch your face when you cum on my dick, Cary."

My dirty words make her mouth fall open into a beautiful "O."

"Off," I give the command and she shimmies out of her dress and then hesitates to unclip her bra. But a cock of my brow has it coming off of her, leaving her in nothing but a skimpy pair of lace undies.

And those have got to go, right fucking now. I lean forward enough to shove my thumbs through the lace and tear them off of her.

I shouldn't have done it, but she'll forgive me. She gasps, but she doesn't protest. Her breathing is coming in short pants and her pale pink nipples are pebbled. She's fucking gorgeous.

I toss them off the bed and grab her hips in my hands, angling her pretty little pussy and taking a languid lick.

Fuck, she's so sweet. Just like I knew my cherry would be. Her fingers spear through my hair and she pushes my face into her pussy. I smile into her tight cunt at how greedy she is. I take her clit in my mouth and suck, making her squirm under me.

She needs more, and I know it. She's trying so hard to get herself off. But she needs me. I massage my tongue on her throbbing clit and I'm rewarded by the sweet sounds of her moans spilling from her lips.

I finally take my hand off her ass and shove two fingers into her pussy, stroking her G-spot and fucking her just like she needs.

"Yes!" she cries out, rocking her pussy into my face. I pull away and pin her hips down, staring at her with a serious expression on my face.

"You need to be a good girl, Cherry," I say and she looks up at me, her breath ragged. "Stop moving your ass, and stay still for me." I'm serious, too. I don't mind her riding my face, but right now I want to be the one controlling her pleasure.

"Yes, sir," she says back breathlessly, and it nearly floors me. Fuck yes. My dick's leaking precum, and I need to get her off quick so I can get inside.

I dive back between her legs and ravage her pussy like a starving man.

Her fingernails scrape along my scalp, but she's holding still for me, even as her back bows with pleasure. *Good girl.*

I suck her clit and push my fingers in, pumping in and out until her thighs are squeezing around my head. I move my face away, licking my lips and looking up her body to find her heated gaze.

"Cum for me, Cherry," I whisper the command, pressing my thumb down on her clit and she ignites under me. Her head falls back as she lets out a strangled cry and then moans my name. She's the most beautiful sight I've even seen. Her thighs are still trembling as I push her legs farther apart so I can fit my hips in between and line my dick up.

I slam into her before she has a chance to come down from her high, and her back arches from the intensity.

I groan in the crook of her neck, completely buried to the hilt and let her adjust to my size. She's so tight.

She's soaking wet for me, but she's so fucking tight.

"Vinny," she moans my name again, and the soft sound spurs me to move. I grip her hips and thrust my own in a rhythmic pace, watching the looks of pleasure play across her gorgeous face.

The dim light in the room makes her soft features look even more beautiful.

"Look at me, Cherry," I whisper as I pick up my relentless pace, nearly out of breath.

She stares back at me, eyes half-lidded and her gorgeous lips parted. "I wanna watch when you cum this time."

She nods her head although she doesn't say anything. She looks like she's lost in pleasure and on edge, and I'm ready to push her over a second time.

I pound into her tight cunt over and over. The bed groans with each thrust and the harder I fuck her, the harder the bed hits the wall. But it only fuels me to take her further, to push her limit higher. I lean forward, nipping her lips and staring into her lust-filled eyes.

My spine tingles, and my toes curl.

Fuck, my balls draw up and I know it's coming. I hold my breath as I fuck her harder and faster. Mercilessly pounding into her and desperate for her to find her release with me.

Her neck arches and her fingers dig into me, but

she never stops looking at me. She's so perfect. Finally, her mouth opens and I hammer into her just two more times and her tight walls are spasming on my dick.

The feel and sounds of her own release push mine over the edge. My body ignites with pleasure, tingling over every inch of skin as I fill her tight walls with my cum in thick, hot bursts. Waves of heated and numbing pleasure crash through my body as she trembles beneath me, shaking from the intensity of her own release.

I lean forward and kiss her sweetly. She moans into the hot air, holding me close to her, and everything in that moment feels right. It settles something deep inside of me, and when I pull away, it's still there.

I don't know what it is, and I try to shake the unfamiliar feeling as I walk to the bathroom and clean myself off before grabbing a washcloth for her.

She's still lying curled on her side in the bed, looking absolutely beautiful and vulnerable with her eyes closed as I wipe up her thighs.

She lets out a small satisfied sound as I clean her up and pull the covers around her. But that action seems to break whatever sensual spell she was under. She sits up with her eyes wide open and looks around the room the second I get off the bed.

She's looking for her clothes. She's already leaving? Damn, that's a first. I try to ignore the feeling in the pit of my stomach.

I walk to the bathroom and toss the cloth in the hamper as she starts gathering her clothing.

"You wanna stay?" I offer. I want her to. I wanna have access to that sweet body all night and wear her ass out.

The thought reminds me that she's working tomorrow. Shit.

Fucking her was a beautiful distraction, but the reality is slowly creeping back in.

"I'll make you pancakes in the morning. Give you a little sausage, too?" I try to make light of it, but I'm already feeling the high wearing off. I wanna just rewind, back to when it was just us enjoying the feel of each other.

"That thing is anything but little," she says comically, looking back up at me as she tosses her torn underwear into the trashcan by the desk.

A grin slips across my face. It's almost like tomorrow doesn't exist. Like what I have planned isn't important at all. But it is. It's life changing. Not just for me, but for those kids.

"So you staying over?" I ask her again. I want her here. I need to keep an eye on her, and I don't like the idea of not having control of that aspect tomorrow.

"I can't. I need to wake up early."

"For work?"

"Yeah," she answers. Fuck. I don't want her to go in. It would be so much easier if she wouldn't.

"I don't think you should." I try to say it teasingly.

"I don't think you should tell me what to do," she says with a smartass tone while slipping her heels back on. Her snappy response makes me walk straight to her and grab that ass of hers, pulling her over to the bed. She gasps as I toss her body down and I cage her in, her small body trapped under mine.

"And what if I want to?" I ask her, staring into those baby blues.

She's breathless and her eyes are heated with desire, but she pulls away. Damn. This time I let her go.

"Sorry, Vinny. I've gotta work tomorrow." She slips out from under my arms, and I groan in disappointment. My dick is so fucking hard again already.

"You gonna leave me like this?" I ask her, gesturing to my obvious hard-on with a grin. "Come on Cherry, I didn't think you'd do me like that."

She gives me a wide smile and leans in, putting her knee on the bed and planting a kiss on my lips.

"Maybe tomorrow?" she asks, vulnerability shining in her eyes. "Late tomorrow night?" She kisses me one more time. "I get off, and then you get off?" she asks, looking straight at my dick.

Fuck, I want that. So damn bad. But tomorrow

night... she might know. There's no way she's not gonna recognize my voice. I gotta figure this shit out.

"You alright?" she asks with concern obviously written on her face and laced in her voice. I realize then that my expression has turned.

"Yeah, yeah Cherry." I give her a small, chaste kiss, my hand cupping the back of her head. "I'll take you back and see you tomorrow night."

CHAPTER 6

CARY ANN

Ever since I grabbed the duffel bag, my heart's been beating out of my chest. I have that ready, along with the tape with the evidence on it. I already wrapped and addressed the tape so all I need to do is mail it, and the video footage has been stopped. I removed that tape altogether and got rid of it, so they'll have no idea it was me. There's nothing stopping me from opening up every register with my PIN number and emptying out the drawers. There aren't even any more shoppers left. For the last twenty minutes this place has been dead. I'm waiting until we're closed though, just in case.

Being open on Christmas Eve is a fucking stupid

thing to do in a small town. Everyone's done their shopping and they're either at the annual parade, or hunkering down and telling their kids Christmas stories as they try to settle them down for bed.

If I wasn't planning on using this situation to my advantage, I'd be pissed that I had to work.

But here I am, prepared to right a wrong and steal this money back. I click the button on my phone and see it's eight. Closing time.

I'm staring at the two cars in the parking lot that aren't mine. They need to leave and get out of here so I can do this and get it over with. I don't know why they're here. Nothing else is open on this strip, and the owners don't seem to be coming in. My palms are sweaty, and my heart's racing. I just want this to be over with. I'm sick to my stomach over it.

I tear my eyes away from the parking lot. I just need to stay calm and do everything with ease.

I close my eyes and take a deep breath, calming myself.

But then my eyes snap open and my heart sputters faster in my chest. Someone's come in. Fucking hell. My nerves can't take this.

I slowly turn, expecting to find Mr. Morose there, ready to thwart my plans because that would be just my luck, but instead it's worse. I'm frozen in place. Fuck. My heart slams against my chest so hard it hurts.

Much worse.

I should scream, but my lungs are paralyzed in my chest, and my legs are shaking. I grip the counter to stay upright as two men in black ski masks walk through the door and the second one locks it behind him.

Oh my God.

I shake my head in disbelief, every ounce of strength replaced with fear. My legs feel weak, and my body feels freezing cold.

"Stay," the first man commands, and some small part of me notes his very deep voice. They each have a gun in their hands, but neither are pointed at me. They have on gloves and masks and all black clothing. Oh shit. No! This can't be happening to me!

My eyes dart to the parking lot as I take in a shaky breath. Both cars are still there. Fuck. I bet they belong to them.

I shake my head, wanting this to all be make-believe.

"It's gonna be alright. You just need to listen and do what we say, and this will all be over with as soon as possible," the man on my left says calmly. His voice is lighter, and sounds more southern.

With the ski masks on all I can see are his deep chocolate eyes. Both men are tall, with broad shoulders. The one on the left is heavier than the other. Internally I start to track all the features that can be used to track these assholes down. I stand a little straighter, feeling my determination come back to me.

I'm not letting them get away with this.

The man on my right slaps a large black backpack on the counter as the man on the left says, "Just put the money in the bag and we'll leave." I stare at the black backpack, feeling the anger rise in my body as my hands ball into fists.

This money was supposed to be for the orphanage. I seethe in a breath through my clenched teeth and shake my head.

"No?" the man to my left says incredulously. He moves the gun from one hand to the other, and while it's still not pointed in my direction, it does the job of instilling fear in me. My heart thump, thump, thumps.

"Look sweetie, it's real easy. You just empty the cash out of each of the registers, or we will."

I shake my head again, feeling tears prick my eyes. The man on the right is stock-still, just staring at me with his pale blue eyes. "I won't give you my PIN," I say in a cracked voice.

This is stupid. It really is. But I can't let them do this.

I can't let yet another person steal from these kids. It belongs to them, damn it! They *need* it. Not these assholes who thought they'd rob a store on Christmas Eve.

The thought makes me even angrier, and I almost

lose my shit. But the man on my right walks closer.

"This doesn't have to be a fight," he says beneath his breath. So low, but he sounds so familiar. He looks to his partner and adds, "We don't wanna hurt you."

Tears leak from the corners of my eyes, rolling down to my cheeks and I angrily brush them away.

"Besides, we've got the key," the man on my left says confidently as he holds up the manager's key. What the fuck? My face scrunches up in a mix of sickness and irritation.

They don't even need my PIN. Shit, I'm going to have to physically keep them away, and that simply isn't going to happen. But I still have to try.

I shake my head and outright refuse. "No," I say with a strength I hardly feel. "I won't let you." I close my eyes and try to summon the courage to continue fighting them.

When I open my eyes, I instinctively take a step back, the small of my back butting against the counter and forcing a small scream from my lips.

Oh fuck, he's pointing the gun right at me, and my heart stops entirely. His chocolate brown eyes stare back at me, daring me to resist further. I put both of my hands up as fear grips me. I don't wanna die. I take in a shaky breath.

"Don't you fucking point your gun at her!" the man on my right snaps. My heart stills, and my hands slowly drop. I do recognize his voice. I shake my head, not wanting to believe it.

But the second he looks back at me, I know it's him.

"Vinny?" I whisper.

CHAPTER 7

VINNY

It's a fake gun, but Toni's scaring the shit out of my sweet cherry. I'm gonna beat the shit out of him.

I'm gonna spank Cherry's ass, too. Money isn't worth putting herself in danger. What the hell is she doing?

I was starting to feel like everything would be fine. We'd just have her step aside, grab the money and get the fuck out.

Easy peasy. I've got the two junkers out front to throw her off, and the cops too once they get here. They can't be traced to anyone, and everything would've been fine.

Shit, I was looking forward to consoling her tonight.

I know my cherry's strong, and she's wanting to do the right thing. But she shouldn't be risking her life like this.

My heart beats faster as she shakes her head no again. She's terrified, and all I wanna do is pull her into my arms and calm her down. I wanna let her in on what's going on. But she's not going to understand. She might not even believe me if I told her the truth.

The very thought that she'd think I was lying and that I'm no good makes my heart hammer faster in my chest.

I can't let that happen. I don't want this to come between us. There's something here, and I want more of her. I can't let this shit get out of hand.

"No," she says as she looks Toni in the eyes. Damn, my girl has some balls on her. "I won't let you."

She closes her eyes, and Toni raises the fake gun in his hand.

Fuck that. He's not going to scare her. I can't let him fuck her up like that. I've had guns pointed at me before. I won't let her go through that shit.

"Don't you fucking point your gun at her!" I scream at him, reaching over and smacking the gun away. I can't hear anything but the sound of my heavy breathing, I'm so pissed. He should know better than that.

I start to tell her to run, to get the fuck out of here before she gets hurt, to do anything but stay here, but she whispers, "Vinny."

My blood runs cold and I stare back at her, slowly facing her and watching the disbelief grow in her gorgeous eyes.

My palms feel like ice. Shit, this is the worst possible outcome.

She knows.

I raise my hand up, trying to calm her as she seems to get over her fear and starts shaking her head even stronger and harder than before.

"It's not what it looks like-" I start to explain myself, but she cuts me off.

"Are you fucking kidding me?" she practically spits out. She must really fucking trust me because all traces of fear vanish, replaced with rage. I was not expecting that. "Are you fucking serious?!" she yells at me.

She's pissed.

"Shit, shit," Toni curses behind me.

"Cherry," I say in a low voice. It's a warning. I know she's angry, but she needs to calm her ass down.

"You aren't taking this money! It's for the orphanage!" she screams as she walks around the counter to get in my face. "You of all people-" she starts to rip into me, but I cut her off, gripping the hand that she tries to shove into my chest. I need to tell her the truth, and she's not gonna like it, and she may not even believe it.

But she's gonna fucking hear it.

"It's not gonna go there," I say as she stands toe-to-toe with me. Completely forgetting the fact that Toni's right there, watching us go at it.

"The hell it isn't!" she yells back. "Take your mask off and talk to me!" She tries to smack my chest with the other hand, but I grab that wrist too and hold her still.

"Stop it, Cherry," I tell her in a low voice, with a threat just barely there. I'm not above grabbing her ass and taking her out of here like a toddler having a damn fit. Toni can handle this on his own. "The video surveillance is running, and I can't let them see my face." I know there's no audio, but there's video at least. I know that much. And even though I know Cherry knows, I still have faith she won't tell them.

"Fuck, man!" Toni yells behind me, slamming his fist down on the counter and pacing a bit. He needs to calm down.

"Everyone, just calm down," I say loud enough for both of them to hear.

"I already cut the feed. You're going to have to fucking kill me." Cherry pulls her hands out of my grasp. "I worked too damn hard to make sure the kids get what they need."

I try to take in what she's saying, but it doesn't make sense. She crosses her arms across her chest, looking at me with tears in her eyes. She's trying to be strong, but the weight of what she just said is wearing down on her.

I tilt my head and ask, "What do you mean you 'cut the feed'?"

She rocks on her back foot and looks away. Fear is creeping in. She's trapped in this store, and she's just said there's no feed. *Cherry*. She really does need me to spank her ass raw. What the hell is my sweet cherry doing admitting shit like that? She's not very good at staying out of trouble.

But then again, if she was, she wouldn't have been with me.

"Tell me." I give her the simple command, and that gets her attention.

"I can't let you steal this money." She says the words simply in a soft voice etched with pain. Conviction is there as well. I know why. She thinks this money is going to the orphanage like it's supposed to. But it's not.

"I'm taking this money to the orphanage," I tell her, staring into her soft baby blue eyes. "Morose is stealing." I take in a heavy breath as her eyes widen. She's gotta believe me. "It has to go there, Cherry. Just let us take it to where it belongs."

She blinks a few times and her breathing comes in short pants. "I swear to you, just let us take it to the orphanage."

"No fucking way," she says, and then my cherry takes

two steps closer to me before she does the last thing I thought she would. She wraps her arms around my neck and presses those sweet lips to mine, moaning into my mouth.

I'm shocked, but she feels so damn good, I fall under her spell, letting her kiss me and setting the gun down on the counter behind her so I can hold onto her small waist, pulling her closer to me.

I could do this all night, but we can't. I try to pull away, but she just holds me tighter. My greedy girl. She doesn't let up until Toni snaps from behind me, "What the fuck is going on?"

CHAPTER 8

CARY ANN

I pull away and look at Vinny's friend. The smile on my face dims as I catch sight of his gun again.

I take another step back and look between the two of them.

"You cut the feed?" Vinny asks me.

I nod my head and reply, "Yeah." My heart is just too full knowing Vinny was doing exactly what I was planning on doing. I feel safe with him. Which doesn't make sense with his friend freaking out. It makes me really uneasy to see the guns.

"What the fuck's going on, man?" The guy pushes on Vinny's shoulder as Vinny takes his mask off.

"She's cool, Toni."

"So you were gonna rob me?" I ask Vinny, ignoring the prickle of fear running through me. I keep looking at Toni. I don't know him, and I don't like that he's here. For some reason it's so easy to forgive Vinny. Especially knowing why he was doing this.

"I didn't want to." He wraps his arms around my waist and pulls me close to him. My small hands land on his chest. "I didn't want you to be scared."

I scoff at him and refuse to admit how worked up I was and say, "I was pissed, not scared." He smiles down at me, like I'm being cute.

I look back at his friend who finally pulls the mask off of his face. He looks vaguely familiar.

"She your girl?" he asks with his brow pinched. "Would've been easier if this was an inside job," he mutters.

He shoves the mask into his pocket and walks over to the nearest register. Vinny's grip on me tightens as I try to pull away and watch Toni.

"So we're robbing this joint together?" Vinny asks me with a smile and then kisses my nose.

I purse my lips, not sure if I trust the fucker at the register.

"It's right across the street, baby. We've got twenty minutes before the parade goes through. We take the cash and slip it through their mail slot in the door." I nod my head. That's better than the plan I had, which was to drop it off in the early morning. Now is better. Get the cash and move it from one place to the next as quickly as possible.

I look at Vinny, and I'm pretty sure I know why he's doing this, but I don't know Toni's story. I watch him as he shoves the money into the bag. Vinny's completely at ease, and obviously trusts him.

"Why are you doing this?" I ask as Toni closes the first register and moves to the next. There are only three in the entire store. So this won't take long.

"I went there once." He looks up at me. He's got a baby face although he's built like a man. "To the orphanage. Without Mrs. Pilcavage I wouldn't be standing here today. There's no doubt I'd be locked up." He opens the next register with the key. "Those kids aren't gonna have the life I had." There's a hint of sadness in his voice.

"You trust me, Cherry?" Vinny asks me, pulling my eyes away from Toni.

"I don't know," I whisper although everything in me does. I shouldn't. I know I'm naive, but I do. I trust him.

"Shoot me, Toni," Vinny says, and my heart stops. Toni laughs and picks up the gun.

"Stop!" I scream out, pushing Vinny hard in the chest, but he's a powerful man and my strength doesn't do a damn thing.

My heart pounds as Toni pulls the trigger over and over again.

It takes a minute for my racing heart to settle. He's gotta be fucking kidding me.

"It's a squirt gun," Toni says before looking at his watch and then heading to the third register, "but there's no water in it."

"I knew you'd be working," Vinny says. "I couldn't bring a real gun, I couldn't risk even the slightest possibility of you getting hurt."

My heart clenches in my chest. I swallow thickly, not liking how strongly I feel toward this man. It's too fast, too soon, but all I wanna do right now is run away with him.

The last register closes shut with a large clank.

"It's not everything that was donated," Toni says, "but it's close." He zips up the backpack and clicks his phone to life.

"Fifteen minutes," he announces, throwing the bag over his shoulders and looking back at Vinny and me. "We gotta get this over there."

Vinny looks down at me, and I know he's going to tell me to stay here. But that's not happening. No fucking way.

"Cherry-" he starts, but I'm not letting him finish.

I shake my head and say, "No, I'm coming with you."

Vinny's eyes are hard, but the moment is broken by the laughter coming from Toni.

"Yeah, she's definitely your girl," Toni says.

Vinny puts his hand on the small of my back and leads me toward the doors as he says, "Let's go then. We gotta make this fast."

"Leave the keys on the counter so they know it wasn't Cherry," Vinny says, and Toni nods. He leaves the keys and then slips a note under them. I walk over and reach down to touch it, but Toni stops me, grabbing my wrist.

"No prints," he says easily, and I nod my head. I suppose they'd run fingerprints on employees first. I could see that.

"What's the note say?" I ask him.

An asymmetrical smile kicks the corner of his lips up. "Merry Christmas, Grinch."

CHAPTER 9

VINNY

She keeps watching Toni and I can practically see the wheels turning in her head. She doesn't trust him.

"Yo, Toni," I call out to him as we walk past the two cars we planted and head through the parking lot to the other side of the vacant strip mall. We drove Cherry's car around the block first. It added on a few minutes to the walk, but I don't want her car out front just in case they find the money gone before Thursday morning. I can't be too careful. It was awkward as fuck driving in the car. She's tense. But she'll be better once this is over with.

The orphanage is close. A five-minute walk if we

step on it, and that's the perfect amount of time. But I don't like the way Cherry seems to be so damn uneasy. The faster we get this shit done, the better.

Toni takes a look over his shoulder, he's leading the way. We have to go this way to avoid the cameras. The direct path goes right through the convenience store, and there's surveillance in that parking lot. So we're gonna avoid that and take the long way around.

Cherry's keeping a safe distance from Toni. I wish she'd knock it off, but she has no reason to trust him.

"Whatcha want, Vinny? I'm not slowing down," Toni answers as he hops over the chain link fence on the edge of the parking lot and turns to wait for us.

It's a clear shot from here on over to the other street.

"Give her the backpack," I tell him. He looks at me with a bit of confusion as I swing my legs over the fence and hop over easily. My sweet cherry is struggling a little. She's on the petite side and I've got my hand out for her ready to brace her body, but she's gripping the chain links of the fence.

"Alright sure, it's a little heavy though." He walks quietly over to Cherry as she tries to right herself. She almost landed on her ass, but I've got a good grip on her waist.

"Here little mama," he says, holding it out for her to take. We're hidden behind the bushes, but as a car passes, we all freeze. No one's out this late on Christmas Eve unless it's to go to the parade on the other side of main street. There aren't any houses over this side of town either. The orphanage is basically on its own on the outskirts of town.

I hold my breath as the car passes, the lights from the headlights peeking through the bushes. I step in front of Cherry and Toni huffs a small laugh at me.

"Calm down, we're home free." He looks relaxed and happy. Truthfully, this is an easy heist. We're so close to being done. I can taste it.

The car passes without incident and Cherry reaches for the bag, her eyes on Toni.

Her expression falls as he drops the full weight in her hand and she hunches forward to get a better grip.

"Holy shit," she mumbles and then shakes her head, shoving the bag back at Toni. "You take it."

Toni looks up at me, and I give him a nod. I just wanted her to see that it's not about the money for him.

It was never about the money. It's about the fact that the town wanted those kids to have a chance. That money isn't for toys. It's for the electric bill, the hot water. It's to put food on the table and shoes on their feet. I know how much those simple things in life can make a difference. And I know that Mrs. Pilcavage is struggling and that she's worried about the money that was supposed to come from the donation, but never came.

My anger rears up inside of me and I lead the way, my hand splayed on the small of Cherry's back. "Let's go," I tell them.

I crouch beneath the low-hung branches of the trees across from the orphanage and look both ways. No one's here, and all but one light in the whole house is off. I look for a sign that someone's watching, but there's no one here and no one looking.

Quickly, we cross the street and head straight over to the side door on the house. The outside light is on, so if someone comes, they'd see us instantly.

"Hurry." Cherry's fear is evident in her voice as Toni swings the bag off his shoulder and quickly starts shoveling the money through the slot. I take Cherry by the waist and lead her in front of him, the two of us blocking anyone from seeing him.

"You look like you're up to no good," my cherry says in a low voice. And I think she's playing with me with that smartass mouth of hers until she pulls on my jacket. Oh shit, I almost forgot about the all black I'm wearing. I quickly shuck my sweater off, I was hot anyway, and toss it into the trashcan out front.

"Toni, you too." He rises from his position, shoving the last bundle through the slot and then the card wishing a Merry Christmas and Happy New Year to all the kids at the orphanage. I know Mrs. Pilcavage, we both do. She's a good woman and when she wakes up tomorrow and sees that money, she's gonna cry with joy and relief. I know she will. It makes me proud to be able to give her back a sense of peace that she gave me all those years ago.

The town clock chimes as Toni stands up and chucks his black jacket off, revealing a beige thermal underneath, shoving the jacket and the backpack both into the trashcan. We toss our gloves and ski masks into the next trashcan and keep walking.

No more evidence. It's done.

I finally feel like I can breathe. The three of us stroll down the street, heading toward the main road where we'll meet up with the parade and blend in. I wrap my arm around Cherry's waist, but she pulls away and runs to a blue metal post office box on the corner of the block. She pulls a small package out of her purse, covered in brown wrapping paper with an address written in black sharpie.

"What's that?" I ask as she drops it into the box. She smiles and says, "The video surveillance of Morose." Pride's written on her face.

I huff a laugh and say a prayer that Morose pays for what he did. At least we've done everything we can do. The rest is in the law's hands.

"You alright?" I ask her as Toni walks ahead. He's got his hands shoved in his pocket and he's breathing easy. I am too, if I'm being honest. Cherry's not, she seems tense and she's looking every which way like someone's just waiting to get us. She gives me a small nod, but I know she's still a little shaken.

I'm a reformed man, but this isn't the first time I've gotten away with this shit. It'll be the last though. I don't need this in my life. Toni turns back to look at us and gives me a nod when Cherry leans against me, wrapping her arm around my waist.

Toni doesn't need it either. This was the last heist for us. It's a good way to end this career.

I look down at Cherry as we stop on the corner, finally seeing the parade just two blocks down. A Christmas elf from the bank is leading the way.

"You think it's going to be alright?" she asks me.

"It's gonna be perfect." I kiss her hair and she seems to relax a bit. "I promise you," I whisper.

The crowd from the parade appears, and the three of us keep on walking. Soon we'll be blending in with them. Just another block to go.

Cherry stops walking as Toni jogs across the road. I turn to look at her, wondering what she's doing.

I look down at my sweet cherry and she points up.

Right above us on a street light is a bit of mistletoe. I

let out a huff of a laugh and look back down at her. She's got a sweet smile on her lips.

"I'll give you that kiss if you stay with me tonight," she says softly.

"You already owe me a kiss," I tell her, cupping her chin in my hand.

"I owe you more than that," she says, batting her lashes. I lean down and take her lips with my own. The sounds of the parade are getting closer, but I don't stop kissing her until we're surrounded and the music and cheers envelop us.

She looks up at me with those sweet eyes when I pull away and I know she's feeling vulnerable and scared, but I'm gonna make everything alright. For her, I'll make it all up to her.

"Merry Christmas, my sweet cherry."

EPILOGUE

CARY ANN

ONE YEAR LATER

"**Y**ou have the biggest smile on your face, Cherry." I hear his voice from across the bedroom. I blush at Vinny as I sit up in bed and rub the sleep from my eyes.

"I'm just happy today," I say easily. I'm so full of warmth and so excited. I love this time of year.

He crawls on the bed closer to me, balancing a cup of coffee in his hand. Peppermint coffee, my favorite this time of year. *Mmm.* I reach out and take the hot mug from him, giving him a sweet kiss before taking a sip.

Coffee is my life source now.

I work nonstop, but I love it. Being a social worker

has made me feel like I'm finally giving back in the way I was always meant to. I feel complete in my career, even more so with Vinny in my life.

My engagement ring clicks on the ceramic mug and the bright light from the morning sun shining through the windows makes it sparkle. Every time I look down at the ring, I feel whole. I love Vinny more and more with each passing day.

Ever since that night, we've exposed ourselves completely to one another. I never believed in love at first sight, but all those years ago, that feeling in my chest was special after all. It had to have been love for us to fit so perfectly together. I know it.

We're gonna start trying to have a baby on New Year's Eve, but the wedding comes first. *A Christmas wedding.* The thought makes me practically shake with delight.

I set the mug down on the nightstand as he curls up next to me, pulling my back into his hard chest. My ass nestles into his crotch and I wiggle a little, wanting him to know that I want him.

I always want him.

His rough chuckle vibrates up my back, and his soft breath tickles my neck.

"Careful what you wish for, Cherry," he warns.

I bite my lip and roll over in his arms.

"So what do you want for Christmas?" I ask him. I

already know the answer though. He told me he wanted to donate toys to the orphanage, so that's going to be our tradition every year. And that's all he wants. Even for our wedding, in lieu of gifts we asked for donations to the orphanage. Especially now that my work deals with a few of the kids there.

No one ever found out what we did last year. We got away without a single soul knowing, and Morose went to jail for the crimes he committed.

Sometimes everything just works out perfectly.

"I already told you," he says softly before leaning in for a kiss.

I smile against his lips.

"All I want is you," he says again, and it makes me feel so full of love.

I brush his hair away from his face and say, "I love you, Vinny."

I whisper the words, and I mean them with everything in me.

He kisses me sweetly and says, "I love you too, Cherry."

About the Author

Thank you so much for reading my romances. I'm just a stay at home Mom and an avid reader turned Author and I couldn't be happier.

I hope you love my books as much as I do!

More by Willow Winters
www.willowwinterswrites.com/books